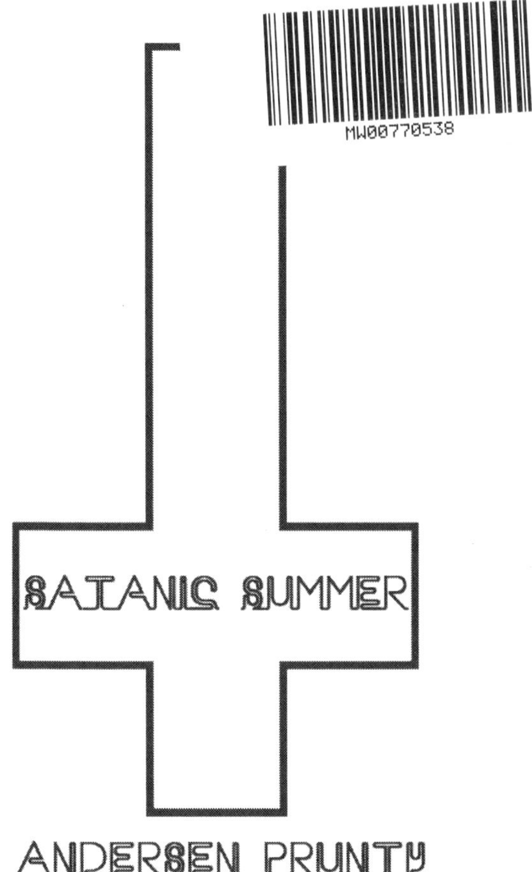

MW00770538
SATANIC SUMMER
ANDERSEN PRUNTY

GRINDHOUSE
PRESS

Published by Grindhouse Press
POB 292644
Dayton, OH 45429
www.grindhousepress.com

Satanic Summer
Grindhouse Press #666
ISBN-13: 978-0-9849692-9-6
ISBN-10: 0984969292

This book is a work of fiction.

Also by Andersen Prunty

Bury the Children in the Yard: Horror Stories

Fill the Grand Canyon and Live Forever

Pray You Die Alone: Horror Stories

Sunruined: Horror Stories

The Driver's Guide to Hitting Pedestrians

Hi I'm a Social Disease: Horror Stories

Fuckness

Slag Attack

My Fake War

The Sorrow King

Morning is Dead

The Beard

Zerostrata

Jack and Mr. Grin

The Overwhelming Urge

Satanic Summer

Friday, June 13th

One

A heavy rain pounded the top of the car. The windshield wipers were virtually ineffective. Even worse, Perry Winthrop had stink hand. Clutching the wheel with his left, he held his right out as far from his nose as he could. It nearly touched the Lexus' passenger-side window.

He squinted his eyes and peered out into the wet darkness. He'd just passed the sign that said he was entering Clover, Kentucky—"A Real Nice Place to Live!"

Some douche bag had changed "Clover" to read "Cloven." *Cause the devil lives in them thar hills, yup!* Perry rolled his eyes.

Clover was *not* a real nice place to live. It was a fucking shithole erected in the foothills of the Appalachians. But he had to be here. Amanda's mom was deep in the throes of dementia and she refused to leave Kentucky. They had a nice house in Hyde Park, on the better side of the Ohio River, meaning in Ohio, but Amanda guilted him into staying in her mother's four room shack.

He hoped the old woman died soon.

Otherwise, he didn't see their marriage lasting much longer. To be honest, the only reason he hadn't divorced Amanda yet was because he didn't want to pay alimony. They'd never had any kids and he was starting to think he wanted it to stay that way.

Perry slowed for a stop sign and rolled on through, knowing there wouldn't be any cars crossing the intersection. Here, everyone seemed to turn in around eight.

Shit.

And it was after midnight.

That was both a good and a bad thing.

It was a bad thing because there was only a certain amount of overtime Amanda would believe he was willing to work. She knew he hated his job. Regardless of how big his salary was, it was only a matter of time before she would stop buying the excuse that he was working until ten or eleven or later every night.

It was a good thing because she would probably be in bed and, therefore, would not have the chance to notice his atrocious smelling hand before he could make it into the bathroom and take a shower. She might even be so asleep she wouldn't notice he'd *taken* a shower.

Undoubtedly, his crotch smelled the same as his hand.

He wanted to stop trolling Vine Street for prostitutes but he couldn't. Amanda didn't have orgasms anyway and, lately, she had claimed to be too tired or stressed out to even try. It was just another nail in the coffin.

He turned onto Mountain Bottom Road. These roads were as shitty as the town. Narrow. No edge markings. Nothing even designating it had two lanes except for the occasional headlights threatening to run him off.

Damn.

His hand really smelled.

The whole car probably reeked.

He made a mental note to buy some air freshener to keep in the car. Maybe some hand sanitizer.

The prostitute didn't look like it had been three months since her last shower. She was actually one of the better looking ones. And one of the more expensive ones. Too bad their pimps didn't have a customer service line. He would have called and begged for a refund. Or a discount on a future fuck.

He took his left hand off the wheel for just a second to crack the window, rain be damned.

He quickly glanced away from the road.

When he looked back up, something stood in the middle of the road.

Perry jammed on the brakes and cut the wheel to his right.

And crashed into the limestone face of the mountain.

"Fuck!"

Airbags were everywhere, shocking him almost as much as the impact with the stone.

His heart kicked around in his chest.

Christ. He didn't need this.

He sat there while the airbags deflated. Opening the door, he stepped out into the pounding rain. Maybe it wouldn't be too bad. Maybe he could just back it up onto the road and continue home. Take it to a shop tomorrow.

What the fuck had been in the road?

At first he thought it was a deer but it seemed almost like it was standing up. There wasn't any sign of it now.

He looked at the front of the car and shook his head.

Steam billowed from beneath the hood.

Busted radiator. Fuck.

The tire was bent under the car.

Broken or bent axle. Damn.

This thing wasn't going anywhere.

He grabbed his phone from his pocket. Hopefully he'd get some reception out here. It wasn't always a given. Jesus. He hated Amanda. Hated her fucking mother. Hated this whole goddamn shitburg sheep fucking town. Hated his stink hand.

At least now he had a somewhat legitimate excuse for being late.

Holding the phone in his left hand, he flipped it open and crouched down, grabbing a handful of wet, muddy grass and wiping his hand with it. While crouched, something ran into his back and he hit the car head first. His phone and his wad of grass went flying.

Anger turned immediately into terror.

What the fuck had just hit him?

He managed to turn around but couldn't seem to stand up.

An excruciating pain shot up his spine and out through his arms.

Rain ran down his forehead and he tried to blink it from his eyes.

Some kind of beast stood in front of him.

It looked like a goat man.

Perry felt an insane desire to laugh.

He asked, "Are you the devil?" but no sound came from his mouth. He held his right hand out like a gun and brought his thumb down, thinking, "Bam!"

The thing approached. Put a giant hand around Perry's and squeezed. Bones popped and ground together.

Before everything went black, Perry looked into the thing's eyes. At first he thought they were red. Then he thought they were orange. Then he thought they looked just like flickering flames.

Then the thing reached out and dragged claws across Perry's throat and he didn't think anymore.

Two

"Dougie!"

The shrill voice clawed him from a heavy sleep.

"You need to get up! I'm gonna hop in the shower!"

His mother, bellowing from the bottom of the stairs. Doug Backus opened his grainy eyes. He looked at the digital clock on his nightstand.

11:30.

Damn. He wouldn't have any time to play *Redemption.*

He had to move quickly.

He threw back the covers. He still wore last night's clothes. He felt disgusting. Dirty. A little hung over. He smelled like sweat.

The sweat of temptation, he thought.

He wanted to turn the computer on just to make sure virtual Doug was still a virgin, that he hadn't given in to the wicked temptations of Sodom City, one of the higher levels of *Redemption.*

But he didn't have time for that. He had to get rid of the beer cans before his mom got out of the shower.

He slipped on his shoes and dropped to his knees. His stomach lurched. He was dizzy and woozy. He waited until he heard the water whistling through the pipes of the house and grabbed the black trash bag of cans and pulled it out from under the bed. The smell of stale beer hit him and he almost lost it. He looked in the bag and counted the cans. Three Old Milwaukee tall boys. He tied up the bag, opened his nightstand drawer, and pulled out a can of strawberry aerosol air freshener. He spritzed the bag and sprayed a cloud throughout the room.

He grabbed the bag and held it away from him as though it were something tainted. He went downstairs and out to the garage. He took the lid off the trash can, lifted the top bag, placed his bag in the trash can, lowered the top bag on top of it, and put the lid back on.

Inside, he paused to make sure the water was still running.

He really didn't feel good at all. He climbed the stairs and quickly ducked into the bathroom off the hallway. He threw open the lid of the toilet and vomited into it, sweaty and shaking.

Fuckin pussy. He heard his friend Crank's voice in his head.

He stood up and flushed the toilet before pissing into it. Then he rinsed his mouth out and brushed his teeth.

He wanted to take a shower but didn't think he had time. He would have to settle for a dense application of underarm deodorant.

Back in his bedroom he put on some fresh clothes. Once changed, he threw open the blinds to his window. Bright, early summer sunshine flooded the room. He was feeling a lot better.

He looked at himself in the mirror on the back of the door. Black greasy hair parted severely on the left. Silver wire-framed glasses that he'd had for the past six years. More acne than he thought an eighteen-year-old should have. The faintest trace of a mustache. Thin plaid short-sleeved shirt tucked into stiff dark blue jeans. Puffy black Velcro shoes.

Doug didn't like the person he saw in the mirror.

He thought about the three beers he still had in his bottom drawer. He didn't know if he wanted to drink them. He had been tempted to drink the beers last night. And he had given into that temptation. Crank, who also worked with him at America Pantry, had told him he couldn't say he didn't like something if he'd never tried it. Just like what his mother used to say about food at the dinner table. Doug wished he could be more like virtual Doug in *Redemption*. Virtual Doug's name was Samuel but he thought it was weird to think of himself with another name, as another person. In fact, he thought it was probably a sin.

"Dougie!"

"What, Mom?!"

"You ready? You don't wanna be late!"

"Coming!" Doug shouted louder than was necessary.

He hated that she always yelled up the stairs. He didn't think it would kill her to walk up the ten steps to his bedroom door. She could probably use the exercise.

He took a deep breath and popped a mint into his mouth, crunching it up. If his mom noticed he had a breath mint in his mouth, she would ask him about it. Maybe it was no big deal, but having to answer mundane questions like that bothered him. Maybe, like the yelling all over the house, the intense scrutiny was just another sign they were the only ones living there.

Doug thought about his dad resting in the urn on the mantel. It didn't look like most urns Doug had seen. It was a large, stainless steel, hollow cross. There was probably only a little ash left in the urn. The rest had been scattered on the infield of the Clover High baseball field. But that was a long time ago. Doug didn't even remember the man.

His mom stood at the bottom of the stairs in a thin muumuu with muted pink flowers on it. The summer heat, *any* heat, gave her the sweats so she liked to wear as few clothes as possible. She jangled the car keys in her right hand.

"Can I drive?" Doug asked.

"Maybe when we have more time. I don't want you to get in a rush."

"But I need the time."

"You'll get time later."

"I'll never get my license."

"What?"

"I said I'll never get my license if I don't get enough hours of driving in."

"That's what we're paying a driving instructor for."

"Yeah, but I need *more* hours."

"You'll get them. Just not while we're in a hurry. I don't want you getting us killed cause you need more hours."

Doug slumped his shoulders and opened the front door. "We could have been there by now."

"What?" His mother always sounded confrontational. He didn't know if she meant to sound that way or not.

"Nothin."

"That's what I thought."

Once in the car, Doug rolled down the window and stared outside. His shirt was already stuck to his back. America Pantry was a gas station and convenience store out on Route 27. Doug watched the tiny town of Clover roll by. A couple of minutes and two stop lights later, they were out of it.

"...on."

Doug had completely fazed out. "Huh?"

"I said the *air conditioner's* on. Roll up your stupid window."

Doug rolled up his window and his mom lit a cigarette.

"Gag."

Doug rolled the window back down.

"Put it *up*."

"Put it *out*."

"No. It's my first one of the day."

"Well, it's *my* first one of the day, too."

"You're such a..."

"What?"

"Never mind." She reached out and turned the air conditioner up higher. Doug flapped his left hand and held his nose with his right.

They reached the station and Doug opened the door.

"Roll up that window."

Doug slammed the door without rolling up the window.

His mother grunted and reached her chubby arms across the passenger seat. Doug opened the door to the Pantry.

Crank stood at the big front window, staring at Doug's mother.

"Look at her, man. She really has to struggle." Crank was barely suppressing his laughter.

"Aw, lay off her." Doug went to the junk food aisle and grabbed a package of Ding Dongs and a bag of potato chips. Then he went to the refrigerator and grabbed a bottle of Yoo-Hoo.

To his right, cans and bottles of beer were lined up like sinister little soldiers.

Doug thought maybe he was going to be sick again.

He hoped he was just hungry.

Three

While Doug ate his junk food, Crank leaned against the counter, furiously texting on his phone. Crank was the complete opposite of Doug. His real name was Stephen. Around their freshman year of high school, he'd started telling people his name was Crank. At first, the kids at school agreed with him and called him Crank because they thought it was funny. But, eventually, the name stuck and the only people who called him Stephen were his teachers and parents. While remaining close friends, it was then Crank's and Doug's interests began to diverge. Doug remained a skinny, gangly dork. Crank developed abs and pecs and biceps, seemingly without any exercise. He pierced himself everywhere, discovered drugs, alcohol, girls, and bands that wore a lot of black and screamed their lyrics.

Currently, he had dyed black hair that looked like it had been run through a lawn mower. Some strands were down to his shoulders. Other areas were shaved nearly to his scalp. It looked like it hadn't been washed in a very, very long time. Since turning eighteen, he had gone to the tattoo parlor on what Doug thought was nearly a weekly basis and now his flesh shone with Satan heads, winged demons, seductively curved women, Egyptian symbols, and various quotes and things Doug didn't care to know the source of.

Doug downed the last of his Yoo-Hoo and stifled a burp.

"You drink that beer you took yesterday?" Crank flipped his phone shut and slid it into his black jeans. He'd worked here longer than Doug and wore one of the gas station attendant shirts. Grayish-blue and pinstriped. Doug noticed the oval patch over his left breast read "Carnk" in red stitched lettering.

"I had a few."

"A few? Weren't those tall boys?"

"Yeah."

"And that's the first time you drank?"

"Yeah."

"Dude, I'm surprised you're not sick... So you must have been pretty wasted. How was it?"

"I don't know. I don't think it's my thing."

"That's just cause you were alone. Alcohol's a social thing."

"If you say so." Doug didn't know if he secretly enjoyed these conversations with Crank or if they just made him nervous. They had always told each other everything.

"You should come out to my house this weekend." Crank lived with his mom in a trailer on some land out on Wickham Road. "We could go out to the woods and drink some more beer. Maybe have a fire or somethin."

"I don't know."

"What else are you gonna do? Sit at home with Mom and play *Redemption* and wait for church on Sunday?"

Doug kind of shook his head but, actually, that was exactly what he would do. And he *liked* it. He liked it all. He didn't care what Crank said.

"Dude!" Crank grabbed both Doug's shoulders and searched his eyes. Crank's eyes were brown and wild, bloodshot. Dark circles oozed from below. "You're fuckin *eighteen*! It's time to take momma's tit out of your mouth. Start living before the adult world steals your soul."

Doug shrugged him off. "That's all just a rite of passage. You'll look back on it—if you live through it—and wonder what the point of it was. You'll develop an addiction, if you haven't already, and probably get some sort of sex disease—"

"I already got crabs from this girl who went to Pendleton County."

"See, maybe you learned a lesson."

"Yeah. I shave my pubes now."

Doug put a hand over his face and shook his head.

"Dude, all you're doing is wasting your time on the computer and jerking off."

"I don't masturbate. You know that."

"Why not?! What's wrong with masturbation?!"

"It encourages sinful and lusty thoughts."

"But you've *done* it?"

"A couple times. I was guilty and regretful afterward. I confessed. I said my prayers."

"Confessed," Crank chuffed. "You're not even a fucking Catholic."

"They still take confessions at my church."

"Right. That church is fucked."

"*Crank*."

"All right. Sorry, man. I just get worked up sometimes. You need to have fun. That's all."

"And I do. In my own way. I know it's not sanctioned by MTV, but I like it."

"You sure?"

"I'm sure."

"But if you ever change your mind, you know I can hook you up, right?"

"You're my auxiliary plan."

"So you gonna drink the beer you have left?"

"I don't know. It didn't taste bad. I would have probably liked it more if it was cold."

"So, you gonna be okay if I go in back and smoke a j before I take off?"

"Yep."

"Patel's supposed to be here around six." Harry Patel was the owner/manager.

"I hope so. I have my first driving lesson. They're picking me up here. So what are you doing?"

"After I smoke the j? Completely alone? By myself? When it would be a much more rewarding experience if my best friend in the world would join me?"

"Yeah yeah. After all that."

"I'll probably go to Chloe's and then to Amber's."

"I thought you were gonna cut one of them out."

"I don't want to hurt either one of them like that. Amber shaves her pussy, which is a real turn on, but Chloe lets me fuck her in the ass. And she has some acid."

Doug felt a red blush crawling up out of his shirt. He couldn't imagine seeing a girl naked, let alone having sex with two of them in the same day. "See, this is why I have to play *Redemption*. So I can feel like I'm actually saving people like you."

"Jesus. A video game where you try to convert people. How fucking lame can you get?"

"At least it hasn't given me crabs."

"Fuck you, Backus." Crank turned to leave and then spun around. "Oh, hey, check out the paper. Some dumb ass ran his car into the side of a mountain last night and got killed."

"Anyone we know?"

"Some guy named Perry Winthrop. I don't know him."

"Where?"

"Mountain Bottom."

The guy's name didn't sound familiar. The road he knew fairly well. It ran out of town and back into the hollow, where most of the people lived in tiny shacks and trailers. He watched Crank wander down the aisle toward the stock room. He turned around and yelled across the store, “The drawer was five dollars over this morning.”

“I know. I paid for the beer.”

“Yeah, well I pocketed it, douche bag.”

Crank disappeared behind the door.

Without Crank around, the job was a lot more boring. Doug sat down on the wooden stool behind the register and flicked on the small TV resting on the back counter.

Four

Crank spent about fifteen minutes in the back room. Doug could hear him coughing all the way up at the register. When Crank finally came out of the back room, he was followed by a cloud of marijuana smoke. He had his uniform shirt unbuttoned and it flapped out behind him as he strolled over to the cooler to grab a bottle of water.

"I'm off!" He flapped his hand in a wave and headed outside.

For the next couple of hours, Doug went back to sitting on the stool and watching talk shows. Only a few customers came in. Teenage jocks and their ditzy girlfriends buying condoms and energy drinks. One of them tried to buy beer and got mad when Doug asked to see an ID. The kid should have known it was easier to just steal it. It wasn't like Doug paid a whole lot of attention and he certainly wasn't going to confront anyone.

Around two, a skinny, twitchy girl came in. She wandered absent-mindedly around the store. Doug stood up from the stool and leaned against the counter, ready for the girl to ask him where to find something. Usually batteries. Nobody could seem to find batteries.

The girl wore an old navy blue sundress that ended above her knobby, bruised knees. Ratty brown Converse with no socks. A dingy cardigan with holes all over it, despite the intense heat outside. Her greasy black hair was pulled back into a ponytail and she wore clunky black-framed glasses. Her complexion wasn't that great. Doug thought she was kind of cute. And he thought he might know her.

She finally made her way up to the counter empty-handed. Her eyes searched behind Doug, roaming over the disposable cameras, tobacco products, condoms, and winning lottery tickets.

"Can I help you?" Doug asked.

"*Yeah...*" She drew the word out. Doug wondered if she was on drugs.

He waited for her to say something else.

"Can I get...?"

She drummed her chipped and badly painted fingernails on the counter.

If Doug were Crank, he would have thrown something by now.

"A pack of Marlboro reds in the box *and...* some condoms."

This was not necessarily an odd coupling of items, but it sounded unusual coming from the girl.

Doug turned around and grabbed the cigarettes, letting his hand hover over the condoms. It loitered over the Trojan lubricated, the most often asked for brand. "Any particular kind?"

"Those are fine."

"These?" Doug tapped the Trojans.

"*Yeah...*"

Jesus, it sounded like she was licking her lips.

Doug put the condoms and the cigarettes on the counter.

"I'll need some ID for the cigarettes."

"Seriously?"

"Seriously."

Disgusted, she reached into the stretched out pocket of her cardigan and slapped her license down on the counter.

"Ha," Doug said, not really so surprised. "Whitney Smith. I

thought it was you. I knew you looked familiar."

She yanked her license back and pocketed it, plopping down some crumpled and moist bills in its place.

"I haven't seen you in, like, four years?" He smiled, trying to be polite, even though he now *knew* she was crazy. And probably also on drugs.

She smirked, making eye contact with him for the first time. "Yep. Four years."

"Where've you been? Did you go live with your dad? I know your mom still lives down the street. When did you get back?"

"I had to go away. That's all. Now I'm back. I just got back yesterday."

Now Doug realized he'd pretty much exhausted their topics of conversation. Whitney grabbed a paper and put it on the counter. "I'll take this, too. I like to read about people dying."

Doug blushed. Like he'd just figured out that Whitney was buying condoms for herself. Probably to have sex with Crank. Everyone was having sex. Doug scanned the cigarettes and condoms with shaky hands, manually punching in the price of the paper and the age verification.

Doug asked if she needed a bag.

"No." Now she wouldn't stop looking at him. He got more and more nervous.

Not knowing what else to say, he said, "You could, uh, come over some time."

"Why? We're not friends."

Doug backed away from the counter and began wringing his hands. "I don't know. I'm sorry. Forget I said anything. That was a stupid thing to say."

"And just because I'm buying condoms doesn't mean I'm easy."

"No. Of course... I didn't..." He turned away from her and sat on the stool before he fell down.

She leaned over the counter and kept staring at him with those nervous gray eyes. Doug fought the desire to look down the loosely drooping neck of her dress. It hadn't looked like there would be much to see there anyway.

"Maybe we'll run into each other sometime again this summer, Doug Backus."

Doug now found that prospect absolutely terrifying.

"Yeah. Maybe." He stared hard at the television, refusing to make eye contact with her.

She grabbed up her things and wandered to the front door and out into the heat. Doug hopped off the stool and watched her from the windowed wall at the front of the store. Surely they wouldn't give someone like that a license. He watched her wander out into the road toward town, thankful she wasn't driving.

The last time he'd seen Whitney was the summer between their eighth grade and freshman years. She was in the same grade as him. The Clover police were pulled up in front of her house. An ambulance was in the driveway and two officers had dragged Whitney out, one of them holding her wrists while the other held her ankles and she thrashed wildly in between. Her mother had stood in the doorway, crying and shaking.

Doug had seen it all but had been unable to figure out what exactly had happened. He had enjoyed speculating about it with Crank and his mother all through the summer. When high school resumed in the fall, it was all their class could talk about for the first week. Some said she had overdosed. Some said she had tried to slash her wrists. Others said she was pregnant or she was really, deeply disturbed. But, like Doug, Whitney didn't exactly have a lot of friends so he doubted the validity of most of these claims. And, since Whitney's mother had become a shut-in, to the extent that Meals-on-Wheels had to bring food to her, no one was getting any truth there. Doug thought the myth was probably more exciting than the truth anyway. And once the football team won their third game in a row, in a season that would ultimately take them all the way to a loss in the state finals, Whitney Smith was all but forgotten.

It took Doug a little while longer but, eventually, he had forgotten too.

Maybe she just needed a little guidance.

Maybe she just needed a little religion.

Maybe Doug had found himself a project.

Maybe Crank was right. Maybe he *had* been playing too much *Redemption.*

Five

Harry Patel showed up at a quarter to six, double parking his black Mercedes in front of the building. Doug knew he hated coming in to work the register but he was too cheap to hire anyone else. From the secret stash located under the counter, Doug figured he liked to watch porn and keep one eye on the door for customers. It was no wonder he hated coming in. Even though he was Indian, most of the town's residents assumed he was using the money he made on the store to fund a terrorist cell. Doug could have told them that what little money the convenience store made was spent on things like the Mercedes, his wife's Jaguar, private schools for his kids, and the homeowners' association fees for the gated community where he lived.

Harry disappeared back into the office and then came up to the front register, wiping the back of his hand across his thick black mustache. "You can go now."

"I don't see him yet." Doug scanned the parking lot for a Chariot Driving Academy car. They advertised themselves as a religious institution. All of their cars had that metal Jesus fish magnet on them. This was good enough for Doug's mom. Doug didn't really see what religion had to do with driving instruction, but he went along with it. It was the only driving school in Clover, aside from the one ran by the high school. Doug was happy to be done with high school and didn't see any reason to go back to the classrooms, even if it was for something that held the promise of freedom.

"You can go now."

"I was going to stay in here in the air conditioning. If you have things to do in the office, I can come and get you when I need to go."

"I'm here. Now I'm just paying you to stand around."

"Ah." Doug nodded his head.

Patel pulled at his crotch and sat down on the stool. Did he already have an erection? His eyes flitted to the drawer containing his secret stash. Doug could tell he wanted to be alone.

"Guess I'll just clock out then."

Doug wasn't even out the door when the sounds of moaning and slapping flesh started up. He felt himself blush.

He waited outside for a couple of minutes before a small, unsafe-looking red car pulled into the lot. This was his first driving lesson and he didn't know what to expect. The passenger side window slid down and a girl who looked younger than him asked, "Are you Doug?"

The girl was extremely attractive and Doug felt immediately panicked. How was he going to be able to concentrate on driving if this was his driving instructor? He nodded.

"Hop in!" she said.

He pulled the door open and sat in the passenger seat. Guiltily, his eyes rolled over the driving instructor. Blonde hair, straight and shoulder length. Blue eyes. Skin tight blue t-shirt stretched over ample but not sloppy or fake breasts. Khaki shorts ending just below the buttocks. Tennis shoes with no socks.

"So, you're Doug Backus. I'm Mindy Astan." She held out a petite hand. Doug took it. His hand was already sweating and he wanted to wipe it off first but thought that would be weird.

"Nice to meet you," he said.

"All right. So we'll do two hours today and count it as four cause I've got some people I'm meeting later. Sound good?"

"Sounds great."

"I thought I'd drive for a bit and you can observe and then we'll get you out on one of the back roads and I'll have you home about eight."

Doug nodded. Observe? Did she mean observe the road or her? Maybe he was supposed to observe the car. His heart leapt around in his chest. She pulled out of the parking lot and he watched her tan, slightly muscled legs work the brake and accelerator. He didn't think she could be any older than him but it seemed like driving instructors had to be at least twenty-one, maybe even older.

"You go to the high school?"

"Just graduated."

"Glad to be out?"

"Oh yeah."

"Most boys are ready to start driving at sixteen."

"My mom made me wait."

"That sucks."

"I guess she thought it would be safer."

"She's probably right. I know I got mine as soon as I turned sixteen and it would've definitely been safer if I'd waited. When you're sixteen, you can't do anything at home so you do everything in your car."

"True." He tried to make it sound like he knew what she was talking about but he really didn't. The only friend he had was Crank and he didn't have a car either, just a dirt bike. "My mom's a little overbearing."

"Aw, she's probably just worried about you. I bet you're an only child, aren't you?"

"Yep."

"And you said you were only eighteen?"

"As of March."

"You look a lot older."

He didn't know if this was a compliment or not.

"These roads really twist and turn a lot. I'll try and find a straight one to get you set up. You can turn the radio on if you want to."

"I'm okay."

"Don't listen to music?"

"Not much."

She poked the volume knob and the radio came on. He expected something more mainstream to come out of it. He didn't know who the band was on this particular song. It sounded kind of like metal but worse, angrier and darker.

The shock must have registered on his face. Mindy reached out to change the station, "Are you not into this?"

"No, it's fine. Really."

She turned the volume down.

He pretended to be interested. "Who is this?"

"I'm not sure. Something foreign. A lot of dots and weird lines over their name."

"I have a friend who's in a band. Their music sounds a lot like that."

"What's the name of the band?"

"Chainsaw Enema."

"Cool name. Who's your friend?"

"Crank? He works at the Pantry with me."

"Oh, I know him. One of my friends used to go out with him."

Doug nodded. He was afraid that, possibly, knowing Crank was not a good thing. Then Mindy's face lit up and she said, "Hey, did you hear about that guy who got killed on Mountain Bottom last night?"

"Yeah. I read about it in the paper."

"My friend Bunt, he's an EMT and he said the guy's guts were all over the road." She scrunched up her face. "He said it didn't look like just a car crash."

"No?"

"No. He said he thinks something got at the body."

"Something?"

"Yeah. Like a wild animal or something."

"Gross."

"Isn't it? You want to go out there? That road's pretty straight. I don't know how someone could run their car off the road. He must have been wasted or something."

Part of Doug was curious. It would be delayed rubbernecking. And he didn't really think he would tell Mindy 'no' in regards to anything.

"So, you want to go there?"

"Sure."

Six

Crank sped along Wickham Road, nothing more than a gravel driveway servicing about five farms. He had the dirt bike opened up, chugging from his forty. Before reaching the driveway to his house, he finished the last of the beer in a single gulp and chucked it off the side of the road. He passed his driveway, en route to Chloe's house. Chloe's house was a cool place to hang out because, since turning eighteen, she had emancipated herself and retreated to the unused barn in the back field. Crank figured this probably wouldn't last much past fall and then she would have to either move back into the house or find an apartment downtown. Of course, she'd need a job if she was going to do that.

He took the left turn into her driveway, the bike wobbling a bit. He was kind of hungry and the beer seemed to be hitting him hard. He gained control, uprighting it, and sped past the house, pulling up in front of the dilapidated barn. He shut the bike off and laid it on its side. Somewhere along the line, he'd lost the kickstand to it. Patel wouldn't even let him keep it in front of the station. He had to store it out back by the dumpster. Crank was pretty sure Patel was hoping someone would either steal it or the trash people would claim it. It was an affront to Patel's upward mobility.

The barn had a large sliding door in the front and a normal-size door to its right. Crank always used the normal-size door, although he thought it would be a really grand entrance to throw back the sliding door. He never knocked. He sauntered in.

The barn actually had a lower level that had once been used to house cattle or horses or something. This was the ground floor level, so it had a plank wooden floor. They'd run electricity out here too but Chloe preferred candles. She sat on the couch she'd dragged from her parents' basement. Some sort of trippy electronic music hummed along in the background. A guy sat next to her on the couch. Crank's heart picked up a little until he remembered he wasn't a jealous guy and had plans to fuck another girl later tonight. The other guy was an interest only. Definitely not a threat. Crank didn't recognize him.

"Hey," Crank said, not knowing if they could even see him.

"Oh, hi Crank," Chloe said. "This is Daniel." She put her hand on the guy's shoulder. She spoke slowly. Crank thought she was probably already tripping. Daniel stared straight forward. His eyes looked black, his skin looked waxy, and he had blond hair spiked up all around his head. A frat version of Sid Vicious. A real douche.

"Hey." Crank nodded. "You got somethin for me?"

Chloe giggled. "I sure do."

She stood up and crossed the floor, pulling up her ragged, too big jeans. When she reached him, she held out her right hand. On the fingertip of her index finger rested a tab of acid. It was black with a white cross on it.

"Nice." Crank took the tab delicately between thumb and forefinger.

"Now..." Chloe straightened her ripped black t-shirt, pulling it over an exposed shoulder. "If you put it on your tongue upside down, you'll have a bad trip but if you put it right side up, it'll be..."

"Yeah, absolutely divine. Fuck that shit." Crank put it on his tongue, never minding which way the cross was turned.

"It's your head." She grabbed his hand and pulled him over to the couch. He'd already gotten what he came for but the beer was still making him feel a little drunk. Maybe he would stick around until it wore off. Find out what this Daniel guy's deal was. Find out if Chloe was fucking him.

He didn't have to wait long for the answer. Chloe went down on her knees in front of Daniel, unbuttoned and unzipped his pants, and pulled them down his hips. She freed his penis from his boxers and it sprung to life. She wrapped a hand around it and began running her tongue along the head. Daniel closed his eyes, his head lolling back.

This guy's a fucking corpse, Crank thought. "Hey, Chloe, I don't know if I'm into this."

She looked back over her shoulder. "Well, you can either take off or hop in or watch. I don't really care. I just want to get fucked before this shit wears off."

Crank was about ready to go hop on the bike, drunk or not, before realizing he was extremely, almost painfully, aroused. Chloe had gone back to sucking Daniel. Crank took in her slender back and the curve of ass. He went down on his knees behind her, pulled her ass to him, tugging her jeans and underwear down to the bend in her legs.

"Good choice," she said.

Crank pulled her ass cheeks apart, spit onto her anus and worked a finger into her. He spit into his palm and slathered that onto his cock. Things were getting a little weird. It was like the only things that existed were him and Chloe and Daniel. He couldn't think of anything besides being inside Chloe. She now had all of Daniel in her mouth. He was grabbing onto the back of her head and pushing her onto him. Crank worked himself into her ass. He watched her hands clench Daniel's thighs with the pain. Crank looked at Daniel's face. His eyes were open now. He was snarling or something. He looked mad. His eyes looked red or orange or something. Acid had always made Crank feel appropriately trippy, but he had never actually hallucinated before. He thought maybe this was a hallucination. The dude had seemed almost comatose a moment before and no one had red eyes, did they? Certainly not this guy. He hadn't ordered the special lenses from some goth site. Not if he was dressed like that. Crank closed his eyes but they didn't want to be closed. He looked down at his cock sliding in and out of Chloe's asshole. It sounded like she was gagging.

The Daniel dude started growling or something and Crank gave him another glance. It seemed like he was being unnecessarily harsh with Chloe, grabbing her head so hard the muscles in his forearms stood out. Crank wanted to do something but Chloe's ass felt so good he couldn't make himself stop. Besides, maybe she had done this with Daniel before. Sometimes Chloe liked it rough.

Crank continued to stare at Daniel. This didn't even look like the same guy as before. His skin looked reddish and it looked like he was growing hair where there shouldn't have been any. Daniel continued to snarl as he thrust into Chloe's mouth. Crank saw long pointed teeth. He was still well aware he was probably hallucinating. Especially when he saw the guy sprout a set of reddish brown horns. Some kind of involuntary noise escaped Crank's throat.

Maybe he wasn't hallucinating.

No. No. He was definitely hallucinating. That's how the fear starts.

But, still, this guy, he's turning into a fucking monster. This could be dangerous.

The voices in Crank's head wouldn't shut up. They kept running in circles. He watched Daniel sprout talons from the tips of his fingers, running them down Chloe's back and shredding her shirt. Crank's heart pounded. His testicles retreated deep inside his pelvic cavity and his penis shrunk and grew flaccid until he was just hammering against Chloe's buttocks.

"Dude," he mumbled.

Then it looked like the guy was reaching for him. His arms

shouldn't have been that long but those talons were right there in front of Crank's face and he could smell the guy or the monster or whatever and he smelled like fire.

"Fuck!" Crank shouted.

He jumped up and turned to run, got caught up in his pants and went sprawling across the floor of the barn. He stood up as quickly as he could and, without sparing a backward glance, pulled up his pants and ran for his bike.

He picked up the bike and hopped on, kicking the starter and finally looking inside the barn. It was semi-dark in there. The bike roared to life. He thought he heard footsteps thundering across the barn floor. But he was already roaring down Chloe's driveway and on his way home. Sweat drenched his clothes and his heart continued to hammer away. Now he didn't feel like he was tripping at all. He felt as sober as he had all day. Had the fear straightened him up that quickly or was it possible he wasn't even hallucinating in the first place?

Seven

Mindy turned onto Mountain Bottom and pulled the car to the side of the road.

"You ready?"

"As I'll ever be."

She put the car in neutral and climbed out. Doug did the same, crossing to the driver's side. He sat behind the wheel. He was nervous and glad this was not a well traveled road. Mindy sat in the passenger seat, stretching around to grab something from the back seat, her shirt straining against her breasts. Doug noticed a shiny silver cross hanging on a chain between her nipples.

"That's a nice cross," Doug said.

"Huh?"

"Your necklace. I like it."

"Oh, thanks."

"Do you go to church?"

"Every Sunday."

Doug immediately found himself even more relaxed. Now there was something he could talk to her about.

"Which one?"

"The Church of the New Covenant."

"Really?"

"Yep."

"That's the church I go to. I've never seen you there."

"Well, I don't actually go to the Church itself. Me and some of the other girls go to the Tabernacle."

"The Tabernacle?"

"Yeah. Haven't you ever heard of it?"

"No."

"It's out in the woods about a half-mile behind the Church. It's an all day thing. A little more intensive than regular services."

"Sounds neat."

"It's great. It really feels like we're doing something important."

"And it's just for girls?"

"Well, women, yes."

"Hm."

Mindy pulled a red motorcycle helmet over her head and flipped up the tinted visor. Doug must not have hid his surprise very well. "I don't take any chances," she said. "If we get into a wreck, I don't want anything to happen to my face or my brain so this takes care of both of them."

"Hopefully you won't need it."

"I'm sure I won't. Okay, we'll take it slow. Have you ever driven before?"

"Nope."

"Not even up and down the driveway?"

"Not even that."

"Oh boy."

She explained to him what he was supposed to do. "Don't worry," she said. "I have a brake over here. Just don't go too fast and I'll stop us before we go off the road or anything."

Doug pressed on the brake pedal and slid the car into gear. He took his foot off the brake and pressed the accelerator lightly until the car crept onto the road.

"You can press it a little harder than that. You just don't want to do it all at once."

Doug did it all at once. The car lurched into the oncoming lane, nearly off the other side of the road. Mindy must have jammed on the brake. She guided him through the reversal process until they were in their proper lane and helped him straighten the wheel. He tried it again. It went a little better. Mindy encouraged him to take it slow. It wasn't as hard as Doug imagined it. He remembered playing a lot of racing video games a few years back. Maybe that helped.

"You're doing great," Mindy said.

"Thanks." Doug glanced over at her. She looked ridiculous in the helmet and delicious everywhere else. She stared straight ahead at the road. His gaze lingered on her nipples and the cross dangling in between. He couldn't believe he'd never seen her at church before. Even if she went to some part of it called the Tabernacle, it seemed like they would have intersected at certain church socials and functions and things. And why hadn't he ever even *heard* of the Tabernacle?

"Look out!" Mindy jammed on her brake. Doug jerked his head back around to the road. The car's tires squealed.

Something huge and hairy darted in front of the car, diving into the woods on the other side and quickly becoming obscured. Mindy whipped off her helmet and placed a hand over her heart.

"What was that?" Doug asked.

"I have no idea. I've never seen anything like it. Could it have been a dog or a coyote or something?"

"It was huge."

"Maybe a deer."

They sat in silence for what felt a lot longer than it actually was, the car idling, both of them breathing heavily. Doug's adrenaline raced. Mindy told him to start driving whenever he felt like it. Strangely, the incident made it easier to concentrate on driving. By the time he was heading back to his house, he felt like he'd grown pretty good at it. And, before saying goodbye, he and Mindy were laughing about the creature they almost hit.

Eight

Crank crossed the living room where his mother slept on the couch looking like a skeleton covered in denim. Must have been another rough night if she was still sleeping it off. He closed the door to his room, sat down on the bed, and started shaking violently. "Fuck fuck fuck shit fuck holy fucking shit. Jesus." He ran a hand through his hair, pulled a cigarette out of his pocket, started to light it, realized that wasn't what he needed, and dug into his jeans pocket to pull out what was left of his stash. That was what he needed. Hopefully it mellowed him out and didn't make him paranoid. Too shaky to roll a joint, he packed the one hitter from his desk drawer and sucked it down faster than he ever had. He held the smoke into his lungs as long as possible and lay back on the bed. As he exhaled, he pulled out his phone and called Doug.

The phone rang three times before Doug's mom said, "Hello?"

"Is Doug around?"

"No. He's taking his driving lessons."

"Can you tell him I called? It's really important."

"Is this Stephen?"

"Yes, ma'am."

"I'll tell him if I remember."

"I'll try back later."

"Make sure it's not too late."

He started to say, "Okay," but she had already hung up on him.

The pot hadn't helped his nerves a whole lot. He was still scared. *Actually* scared. Once he was away from the jock bullies at the high school, he didn't think he would ever be scared of anything again. Especially not of anything as ridiculous as... as...

Monsters.

Was that what it was?

He had to have just been hallucinating. People can't do that. Change shapes right in front of him. What the fuck? Now he almost wanted to laugh, it seemed so ridiculous. What did he think the monster was, anyway? The Devil? He'd have to stop listening to some of his music if it started making him think of shit like that.

He could just call Chloe.

But she probably didn't want to talk to him after running out like that. It had to be embarrassing. Hell, *he* was kind of embarrassed. Especially if it turned out to be nothing. He'd actually been so scared he'd lost his erection. That had never happened before. He'd never even thought of it before. What if he wouldn't be able to have sex anymore? What if he always thought of that?

Okay. He tried to reason with his conscience. He needed to call Chloe. So what if it was embarrassing. Less than a half hour ago, he'd been fucking her in the ass while she was sucking off a practical stranger and they were all tripping on acid. There didn't seem to be any reason for shame or embarrassment.

He pressed the '6', speed dial for Chloe, and chewed his bottom lip while the phone rang. Once he was sure it was about ready to go to voice mail, she said, "Crank?"

"Yeah. Chloe?"

"Um, *yeah.*"

"I was just calling to make sure you, uh, you're okay and everything."

"Why wouldn't I be?"

"No reason. It was just strange, that's all."

"Only strange if you're a fucking puritan who can't keep it up and gets freaked out by things like that."

"Things like..."

"Me and another guy. What else? You know if the situation had been reversed, I would have been cool with it. I've practically begged you to bring Amber around but..."

"Oh, yeah..." He tried to laugh it off. "Sorry about that. Maybe next time, huh?"

"I'm glad you called, Crank. I was actually going to call you a little later."

"Yeah. What for?"

"To tell you there wouldn't be a next time."

"What?"

"You heard me."

"Come on, Chloe..."

"You blew it, asshole. I'm with Daniel now. He's all I need. Maybe with him I won't need to feel like I need more."

"Certainly seems like you wanted more a while ago."

"It's over, Crank. Please don't call me anymore."

"Fine. You're a fucking hog anyway." Crank pressed the end button and tossed the phone toward the foot of the bed.

Bitch.

Crank slunk down on the bed and closed his eyes. He felt relieved. Just like he had thought, it was nothing. Just a hallucination. So what if Chloe didn't want to see him anymore? He could live with that. As long as there wasn't a monster out there. That was something that caused him a great amount of anxiety. But now he could forget about it. Girls were the real monsters.

He drifted off after a few minutes.

Nine

Doug walked in the door to find his mother asleep on the couch with the TV at top volume. He thought about waking her up and then decided he didn't want to talk to her. He took the cordless phone up to his room and called Crank. He had to tell him about nearly hitting the animal out on Mountain Bottom. Crank didn't answer his phone. He briefly thought about calling Whitney and then wondered why she would want to talk to him. She had made it pretty clear they were neighbors and nothing more. He didn't know why he would want to talk to her anyway. She was crazy, after all. That hadn't seemed to change over the years. She wasn't even particularly cute, yet he found himself wanting her to come to the station again. Maybe she was a chain smoker and the cigarettes wouldn't last much through the night. Maybe she was a chain fornicator and would have to get more condoms.

What if she came to the store while Crank was there?

She wasn't really Crank's type though.

Wait a minute, he corrected himself. Every girl was pretty much Crank's type. He had never met a less discriminating individual.

He turned on his computer and logged in to *Redemption.* If he could survive the sordid streets of Sodom then he might earn the golden cross. Just one level away from the golden crown. He didn't know what he would do if he won the game. Hopefully, they would come out with a new version soon. Or maybe he could play it again and be one of the sinners. That could be kind of fun. To fornicate with all the whores and sluts that populated the game. But what fun would that be? They were just images on a computer. The person on the other end was probably someone like him. Or some fat middle-aged guy who was afraid to leave his house. Or someone like Whitney.

That made him put the thought out of his head. He reminded himself it would be a sin to approach the game in that way. Even though that may be what the evil video game designers, undoubtedly hailing from some hotbed of sin and lust like California, wanted, he wasn't going to give in. He knew that was the secret of the game. That was why it was one of the few forms of popular entertainment endorsed by the Church.

"Dougie! You home!" His mother shouted up the stairs.

"Yes!" he screamed toward his closed door.

"You got the phone!"

"Yeah, Mom!"

"I need it!"

He slumped his shoulders, picked up the phone, opened his door, and tossed it out onto the stairs. Cigarette smoke wafted up. He slammed his door.

"Coulda brought it down!"

"I don't wanna get cancer!"

He heard her grumbling and went back to playing his game. He thought about the beer in the bottom of his drawers and decided he would wait until he knew his mother was in bed. Tonight, he would take the cans and hide them in the trash can as soon as he was finished so he didn't have to worry about doing it in the morning.

He achieved the golden cross around midnight. He had heard his mother's snores start around ten and, after about a half hour of that, he pulled the first tall boy from the drawer and downed it within a few minutes. It made the game even more fun. It made fighting off temptation even that much more difficult. Still, he had managed. And three beers later, he had the golden cross and felt like he was going to pass out. He went downstairs to the garage and hid the cans in the trash, put the phone back on the charger after wiping down the mouthpiece, noticed there weren't any voice mails, and went back upstairs. He didn't even take off his clothes. He lay down in the darkness, listening to the summer sounds outside his bedroom window and thought about Mindy and Whitney and that awful thing they had seen on the road. He remembered how Mindy had said the guy who had died had looked like he was mauled by some kind of wild animal. Could that have been the wild animal? Who knew? His next lesson was tomorrow after work and that already seemed too far away. It wasn't as hard as he thought it would be and Mindy was really fun to be around. Not to mention that she was about the most attractive girl he had ever seen. His penis was very stiff in his jeans. He thought about masturbating and then he thought about going to hell to burn for all eternity and then, finally, he fell asleep.

Ten

Angie thought Jim Lankmeyer was taking his Christ adulation way too far.

"I don't see why we can't just fuck like most normal people."

He was crouched down, pounding the final nail into his makeshift cross. He whipped his head back over his shoulder and hissed, "Because that is a *sin*, Angie."

"Something tells me this is probably a sin, too."

"I haven't found any evidence of that. Where is Christ if we are having sex? Nowhere. That's where. This will be beautiful. This is sacrifice. I will put myself in Christ's place and feel what he felt."

He handed the hammer to her. She let it rest against her shoulder and rolled her eyes. "It just seems so sick and wrong."

"I know what you did with Elliot Beerman. I heard all about it. I know you like to hurt people. I know you like to cause pain. This should be right up your alley."

"You know what else I like sometimes? A cock in my vagina. That feels good. You might like it too if you'd give it a try."

He stood up and stood very close to her. "Not until I am married under the eyes of God."

"No fun."

"Why do you have to be so difficult?"

"Because this is dumb. That's why."

"Do you think you can lift me up if I lay down on it?"

"I can try."

"Okay."

Jim lay down and spread his arms out on the cross. Angie rifled through the toolbox until she found the big, thick nails the sick bastard probably bought just for this occasion. She really wished she lived in a city. All this nothing. All this nowhere. It caused people to do things like this. She was in her early twenties and didn't think this was how she was supposed to spend a Friday evening. But she stuck around. Just like everyone who went to the Church of the New Covenant, or the New Cov, as they said when they wanted to try and make it sound cooler than it could ever be. Something was going to happen. If everything Pastor Don said was true, something was happening right now. But soon—SOON—something really, really big was going to happen. She had made a pact with herself to give it another year and then she thought she would have to get out.

Jim cast his eyes toward the big moon and took a deep, shaky breath. "This is all for you," he whispered. "Lord Jesus, this is all for you."

Angie rolled her eyes. She lowered herself onto his hips in a blatantly sexual position. She was curious to know if he was hard over this. He gave her a disparaging look. "What? How else am I supposed to do this?"

She wore a black skirt and liked the feel of the lump in his jeans pressing against the thin layer of her underwear. "So I just pound them in?"

"Yes. Try not to pound them into any bones."

"Are we doing the feet too?"

"I don't think that will be necessary."

"It might give you some support. You never know. You don't want any tearing."

"That's why I've put the foot rest on the bottom. If a nail through my feet is necessary, then we will drive the nail through my feet."

"Jesus probably didn't have a foot rest."

"Angie."

"I'm just sayin." She took a deep breath. At first, she didn't know if she could do this or not but it was one of those things that became so absurd she felt like she had to. Her friends would enjoy hearing about it anyway. "Left hand first?"

"It doesn't matter."

"Are you sure you don't want some painkillers? I have some pretty decent stuff in my bag."

"That is not necessary. I will absorb the pain and turn it into Christ love."

"Ready?" She steadied the nail in her left hand, reaching over his body, her crotch resting snugly against his. She was pretty sure she felt something there. With her right hand, she swung at the nail head, missed, and smashed his middle finger. He gasped sharply. "Sorry." Jesus, he was even harder now. On the next swing, she connected with the head of the nail and it went most of the way through his hand. He bucked his hips against her. She was pretty sure he was crying. But he had told her not to stop under any circumstance so she gave the nail a couple more blows until it met wood. She continued pounding until the head was flush with his bloody palm. He was relatively quiet and she wondered if he had passed out. Looking at his face, she could see the tears streaming from the corners of his eyes but the eyes themselves were upturned rapturously. He kept muttering things like "yes" and "Lord Jesus" under his breath. This was becoming more and more like sex.

"The other one now?" she asked.

"Yes. The other one now."

This one went more smoothly. By the time she was finished, he was breathing heavily, almost panting. Now she was to stand him up against the huge tree and leave him there until morning. She knew that, even though he said he was doing all of this to prove his love for Christ, he was actually doing it so he could go to church on Sunday morning and show Pastor Don his hands and try to convince him he had stigmata. It was like a race with the men in the Church to see who could be the holiest. She didn't know why women were never included in this. If there was such a thing as the second coming of Christ, wasn't it possible that it could be a woman? Or did that go against some type of family values?

Oh well, she knew the secret of the Church anyway. She wanted to laugh at all of Jim's false piety.

If he only knew.

If so many of the parishioners only knew.

She stepped up to the top of the cross. She guessed, maybe, it was a crucifix now. She made sure to step directly over Jim's head, affording him the perfect chance to see up her skirt. He probably didn't care. She bent over and put her hands under the crossbeam.

"I don't know if I'm strong enough to do this."

"It is Christ's will, Angie. Of course you will be able to do it."

She lifted and managed to raise it off the ground with no problem. She didn't know if it was Christ's will or if Jim just wasn't really that heavy. He probably only outweighed her by about thirty pounds. She gave the crucifix a yank and let it come to rest against the tree. She now stood in front of him and pushed the crucifix up higher. She walked back to her bag, resting beside the toolbox, and pulled a length of rope out of it. She held it up in front of Jim.

"I thought you would probably want your feet restrained in some way. Since you didn't want to be like Jesus and have me put a nail down there, I thought this rope would do."

"That was an excellent idea, Angie. But I don't appreciate your derision."

"I'm not deriding. I just thought it would be a good idea."

"Then do it. That will ensure that I do not tip the cross over and walk to seek help."

"I thought I would be staying here with you."

"This is between me, God, and his son."

"Suit yourself."

She tied the rope around his ankles. Secure, but not tight enough to cut off the circulation. She backed up to look at him. He continued to stare up at the sky. He wasn't a bad looking guy. She knew he wasn't a virgin. He was one of those "born again" virgins. The type of guy who did his hard living in high school until they almost died or something and then his brain was so fried he decided to start going to church and do things like this. It still came down to the same macho posturing bullshit, Angie thought. She took a step toward him. She unbuckled his belt.

"Angie? What are you doing?"

She unbuttoned his jeans. Unzipped them. Slid them and his tighty whities down to his knees. His penis was very erect. It wasn't huge but it seemed to be at maximum volume.

"Angie. This is not a game. This is not some kind of sex game. I don't know what I've done to give you that idea."

"Just, uh, think of Jesus or something." She went down on her knees. She touched her tongue to the tip of his penis. Wrapped a hand around the base. Used the other hand to cup his scrotum.

"This is practically rape, Angie. I'll tell Pastor Don of your paganish ways."

She laughed softly, eyeing his stiff cock. "Yeah, you go ahead and do that." She ran her tongue down the length of his shaft and the next thing she felt was a ropy strand of warm semen coursing down her cheek. She rolled her eyes and wiped it away. Stood up. Her fun was over.

Unless.

Unless she just left him like this.

She began backing away. She waved and smiled sarcastically. "Night, Jim." Then she turned and darted off into the woods.

He had never felt this much shame before. His face burned with the heat of the summer and embarrassment. Who would find him in the morning? Who would find him like this? His penis hung limp against his scrotum, a rope of semen trailing out. That was the bad part. The semen. It cheapened everything. Now whoever saw him, whether they believed what Angie had done to him or not, would think this wasn't pure. Would think tonight's activity had been fraught with lustful thoughts.

The woods and dead leaves were suddenly alive with sound.

His face continued to burn with shame. He even thought about trying to free his hands just so he did not have to face the dispersion that would be cast upon him.

Who would find him like this?

Would it be mean high schoolers or someone from the Church?

The ground seemed to rumble with the force of the intruder. Maybe it was some kind of wild animal. A really large wild animal. Maybe it was just a wild horse. Maybe it was a bear. He'd never heard of bears in these parts but... anything was possible.

What he saw was none of these things.

It stood in front of him, covered in reddish fur, giant horns gleaming under the moonlight.

Angie. Angie's harlotry had summoned the Devil.

"You don't want me," Jim said. "I am pure. You want the girl."

The beast sniffed the air and moved closer to Jim on cloven hooves, its tail swishing back and forth. It leaned toward Jim, lowered its head to his crotch, sniffing.

Jim started to pray.

The beast took a great bite and bathed in the blood.

Eleven

They had just finished taping the last of the black trash bags to the living room wall when the door bell rang.

"That's probably them." Mindy walked toward the door and opened it up, the humidity immediately assaulting her. A man in bib overalls stood illuminated in the porch light, moths flapping around his head. "Are you from Baal's?"

The man didn't say anything. He shrugged and looked down at the goat to his left.

"I guess so."

He spit out some tobacco juice to his right and produced a clipboard with a contract on it. "I'm gonna need you to sign here."

Mindy took the clipboard, gave the contract a cursory glance, and signed at the bottom with the man's greasy pen. She handed the clipboard and the pen back to the man. He tore off the carbon copy and handed it back to Mindy.

"It's all yours. No returns."

"I don't think that will be a problem."

"Never is."

Mindy took the goat by the collar and shut the door as the man turned to head back to his black cargo truck. Once inside, the goat unleashed a torrent of urine, spattering against the plastic of the trash bags.

"Yuck," Kristen said. She looked away from the pentagram she was spraying onto the wall with glow-in-the-dark paint. "Why do we have to use my house?"

"Because your parents are gone."

"This is creepy. And gross."

"We're just doing what we were told. There will be rewards. You know that."

"I know. This just isn't how I thought I would be spending Friday nights once I got out of college."

"But you didn't graduate from college. You're graduating from the Tabernacle and this is one of the things we have to do. It will all be over soon and then the Kingdom will be in Clover. We'll be a Mecca for the entire country."

Mindy let go of the goat. It bucked its hind legs, shat on the floor, and moved to the other side of the room. Kristen finished the pentagram. Mindy put a hand on her left elbow. "Come on," she said. "You know it's worth it."

Kristen turned around and met Mindy's intense gaze. Mindy moved in and kissed the other girl on the lips. They moved closer to each other, their tongues darting in and out of each other's mouths.

"I guess you're right."

"Now let's finish getting it set up before he shows up."

Kristen commenced to painting some more pentagrams and upside down crosses on the walls. Mindy lit several candles. The goat slept.

Soon they heard the beast at the door, something between a pant and a growl. Kristen rushed over to open the door before the beast busted it down. He would be hungry and sometimes that made him destructive. The beast rushed in, huge and stinking. Kristen quickly shut and locked the door. The worst thing in the world would be for someone to walk in on them in the next few hours.

The next few hours, she mused. That was why they had come to love the beast. He could make them feel things no one else had.

The beast couldn't talk when he was like this. Too many teeth. Too many primal desires surging through his body. He growled and held out his arms. His hide was damp and dark and Mindy wondered if he was already soaked in blood. She moved close to him and he grabbed the back of her head, pulling her into his chest and then forcing her mouth open. He wanted her to lick his fur. To suck the blood from it. She wondered who the blood had come from. She licked and sucked a clump into her mouth until the rich taste was gone. Then she pulled away from him and said, "We've brought you a present, Lord. Kristen, the goat."

Kristen picked up the curved ceremonial knife from a trash bag covered end table. She approached the sleeping goat. She straddled it, grabbed it by one of its horns and lifted its head. Its eyes shot open and she dragged the knife across its throat. It began bucking and twitching, its blood spurting out, darkening its coat, pooling on the floor. Kristen forced it to the ground. It continued to bleed on the floor, its twitches becoming slower. The beast and the two girls approached the puddle. The girls stripped off their clothes and dropped to their knees, bathing in the still warm blood. And then the beast pulled both of them to him and forced their mouths to move over him. His penis became larger and harder. And, once they were all full on the blood of both human and goat, he reminded them why they were both so devoted.

This continued until nearly dawn, when he disappeared back into the humid night.

Mindy and Kristen fell asleep in each other's arms.

Saturday, June 14th

Twelve

Crank had awoken sometime after midnight. He was terrified but reminded himself everything was okay. He convinced himself he hadn't seen what he thought he saw. He needed something to do to take his mind off it. He went into the bathroom of the double wide and got the hair scissors. Then he went into the kitchen until he found some tape. He went back into his bedroom, huddled in the corner and cut off chunks of his greasy hair. He picked the clumps of hair up from the floor and began taping them to his left arm. He checked his cell phone to see if he had any messages. It looked like Doug had called but it was too late to call him back now. He wished it wasn't dark outside. He wished a lot of things.

Chainsaw Enema was playing a show this coming Friday. Less than a week away now. He tried to think about that. He downed most of the King Cobra forty under his bed and passed back out, thankful that tomorrow he didn't have to go in early.

Thirteen

"Doug! *Dougie*!!!"

Shrill and relentless, his mother's voice. What time was it? Too early. He could tell without even looking at the clock.

"Doug!"

It was like someone was being murdered or something. His head was reeling. He felt like throwing up. He was sweaty, still wearing last night's clothes, and lying on top of his comforter. The monitor to his computer was still on.

"Doug!"

A brief moment of panic when last night came back to him. He remembered stashing the beer cans in the trash can. He had nothing to worry about. Hopefully. He finally looked at the clock, hoping he wasn't running late but not really caring, either.

"Doug! Get down here!"

It was only three after seven. He didn't have to be at the station for nearly another hour. He got out of bed, his clothes feeling damp and stretched out. He opened his bedroom door and walked down the stairs, moving very slowly. His mother stood at the bottom of the stairs, red and panting. He wanted to find out what the big deal was but he also needed to urinate and throw up. He walked past his mother, making straight for the bathroom.

"You have to tell me what this crap is," his mom said.

"Let me use the bathroom first."

She furiously jammed a cigarette between her lips and lit it.

Doug went into the bathroom, closed the door, turned the water on full blast, urinated, vomited, and then flushed the toilet. He washed his hands, brushed his teeth, and splashed some water on his face. He wondered if he still smelled like beer. He felt like it was seeping from his pores. His mother would know. She'd be able to detect the faintest trace of it. But now he was kind of trapped.

She stood on the other side of the door when he opened it. Her cigarette was already nearly gone, smoke curling around her head and shooting from the corners of her mouth.

"Why'd you leave the water running? Are you bulimic?"

"No, I... I'm not feeling well is all."

"Well first you have to come and look at this crap on the front porch."

Doug wondered, momentarily, if maybe someone had actually placed some variety of feces on the porch. He followed his mother to the front door, which had been left open. She pointed down to the offending item and said, "See there. What is it? And why did someone leave it there?"

Looking down at it, he had no idea what it was. He knew what it was made from and it only took him a couple of seconds to realize who had *probably* left it there, but he had no idea what it was supposed to actually *be.* It was, vaguely, a cross. Two Old Milwaukee tall boys made the body and two more jutted from each side to make the arms. A condom had been blown up and placed on top. He could tell it was a condom because of the reservoir tip. While he had never had any personal use for condoms, he had seen them lying around on the trails in the reserve and in Crank's bedroom. One of Doug's old school pictures—black and white and presumably cut out from one of the yearbooks—was glued to the condom. Cigarette butts formed its fingers, toes, and something that Doug guessed was supposed to be a loincloth.

"What is it?" his mother repeated.

"I don't know."

"Who would do something like that?"

"I don't know."

"Was it Stephen? It seems like something that little punk would do."

"It probably wasn't Crank."

"How do *you* know?"

"Well, for one thing, Crank is way too lazy to do something like that."

"It looks evil."

Doug wasn't sure what it looked like, but he didn't think it looked evil. Maybe just because it was cruciform in shape, he thought it looked more religious than evil. Except that his photo glued to what should have been the face seemed to portray him as Christ or something, which was probably a sin.

"Do you think we should call the police?"

"That's probably not necessary."

"Maybe we're marked or something. Maybe whoever did that is going to come back and do something worse."

"I don't think anything like that's going to happen."

"These cigarette butts are my brand. I think whoever did this went through *our* trash can."

"Tons of people smoke Marlboros. Where did they get the beer cans? Where did they get the condom?"

"I don't know, Dougie, I just don't know... They're not... *yours* are they?"

Doug laughed and hoped he didn't sound too nervous. "Of course not. Wouldn't you *know* if I was doing anything like that? I mean, you're always here."

"I just don't know," she said again. "We need to get rid of it. We need to put it back in the trash. I don't want to touch it."

"I'll take care of it."

Doug's mom went back into the house. Doug picked the thing up and carried it around to the door at the side of the garage. He actually kind of liked it. It was like some kind of totem to vice. He wondered if the condom was used or not. He held the totem up to his face and sniffed it. He wondered if it smelled like vagina, not that he would know. He just thought it smelled like latex and it made him think of sex as a clinical act and that made him sad. He took the lid off the trash can and gently placed the totem on top. He intentionally picked the fuller of the two trash cans, hoping his mom wouldn't put a disgusting trash bag on top of it. He thought he might want to study it a bit later. He went inside to take a shower and change clothes before his mother took him to work. Hopefully, she wouldn't keep dwelling on the totem.

Fourteen

The only thing she had said about it on the way to Patel's was that it frightened her and she was going to pray for whoever had created that "awful, evil piece of blasphemy."

Entering America Pantry, Doug found Patel asleep on his back behind the counter, one hand shoved down the front of his pants. Doug thought it would be awkward to wake him up so he went around the store and straightened up the shelves. He wondered how long Patel had been asleep. It was probably good Clover was such a low volume market. Otherwise, the shelves would probably be looted and bare. He looked at the heavily pilfered beer cooler with something like longing. He was out. He thought he wanted more. He wished Crank was working today. Doug wouldn't take any, even if he paid for it because he wasn't twenty-one and, therefore, it was illegal. Of course, the consumption of alcohol if you were under twenty-one was technically illegal too. But, he reasoned, that was only in certain parts of the world. He was sure he'd heard that entire families, regardless of age, enjoyed wine around the dinner table. Maybe he was just a hypocrite. Or maybe he just didn't want to get caught.

A sinister-looking man in a black leather trench coat entered the store. Doug retreated behind the counter. The man brought up a bottle of Tahitian Treat, maxi pads, and aerosol cheese. Patel began to stir as Doug rang the man up. He paid cash and strolled out of the store. Doug didn't see him get into a car. He seemed to vanish into thin air. Doug fought the urge to dart out and see if he could see him anywhere outside.

Patel stood up and straightened his hair, wiped some drool from his chin, and backhanded his mustache. He pressed a button on the TV/DVD combo and took the disc out, putting it in a plain black case and throwing it into his special drawer. He crouched down to lock the padlock and said, "I'm going now."

"Want me to count the register?"

"Okay." He was already heading for the door.

"I have driving lessons again tonight at five."

"Someone will be here."

Then he was gone. Doug kind of hoped it would be Patel's wife, who was a lot younger than Harry and kind of cute, and infinitely more pleasant. She was probably closer to Doug's age than Patel's.

Doug took a deep breath and sat down on the stool. It was going to be a long day. His thoughts turned to the totem and then to Whitney Smith. He was pretty sure she was the one who had constructed it. He wondered why. It seemed bizarre. Although, he reminded himself, Whitney may not be the most stable person in the world.

He thought about calling Crank but figured it was way too early. He needed to get a laptop so he could play *Redemption* here.

That would make the time pass.

Around one, Crank strolled in with a blonde, hippie-looking girl who wore cut-off denim shorts, a tank top, and seemed absolutely bursting with ripeness—Amber. Crank had described her as the one who shaved her pussy. Doug tried to force the image out of his head.

Crank walked to the counter. "What up, Doug?"

"Not much." Something seemed off with Crank. Doug wondered if he was on something strange or if he just had a rough night.

"Called you last night."

"Driving lessons. Remember?" Amber's nipples jutted against the fabric of her shirt, large and balanced perfectly on her young full breasts. She vacantly batted her eyes at him.

"Yeah yeah. That's what your mom said. Patel around?"

"Took off a while ago."

"I'm gonna take Amber to the back and bang her." Amber lightly punched him on the arm and rolled her eyes. "Wanna watch?"

Doug felt himself blushing. "How can I answer that? Do you *expect* me to answer that?"

"Yes or no would do, I guess. You're probably insulting Amber if you say no, though."

Doug looked at Amber. "No offense but no."

"Hey," Crank said. "I told Doug about your pussy. Show him."

"Uh, no thanks."

"Come on. You'd like to see that, wouldn't you, Doug?"

Doug couldn't answer. He would have liked to see. Just thinking about it took all the air from his lungs.

"See, he can't even talk. Toss me some condoms, brother?"

"You gonna pay for them?"

Crank waved dismissively. "Yeah yeah. *Later.* I want to test them first. See if they're worth it."

Doug slid the Trojan lubricateds across the counter.

"You comin over tonight?"

"I have driving lessons again."

"How bout after?" Crank darted an almost indiscernible look at Amber. "You really should. I got something I want to ask you."

"I'll try. I might be tired. And Mom would have to take me."

"Just have the driver guy drop you off at my house. I'll get somebody to take you home."

"It's a woman, not a guy and, like I said, I'll see."

"All right. But you should come. Watch us practice. Let me know if we suck or not."

Doug wondered if this was really important to Crank or not. He thought they were supposed to suck.

Crank grabbed Amber and turned her around. "I'm gonna go unload some chowder."

They walked toward the back room. Doug watched Amber's butt move beneath the denim of her shorts. He wondered how it would feel to put his hands on it. He thought about her shaved vagina. Then he wondered why Crank had hair taped to his arm. Something was up. He thought he probably *would* try to make it to Crank's tonight just to find out what the deal was.

Whitney came in a couple of hours later, just as Doug was sliding into some kind of mid-afternoon coma. Crank and Amber were still in the back room. When she came in, Whitney made brief eye contact with him before looking away, around the store, up at the lights, wandering aimlessly around and dazedly reaching out to touch certain things.

Finally, empty-handed, she made her way to the counter. Doug wished he had brought the totem with him so he could now place it in front of her and see if it got any kind of reaction. She placed her bony hands on the counter. Her fingernails were covered in chipped black polish and looked gnawed. He thought the smoking would have helped with that. Her eyes searched the racks behind him.

"Whitney." He tried to keep his voice as icy as possible.

"Doug."

"Would you like the usual?"

Now she made eye contact with him. Her eyes seemed to bounce around in the sockets. He thought she looked cleaner today. The sweater was gone and she wore a baggy white t-shirt. Still, he could see her raised nipples through it. He wondered why everyone's nipples seemed noticeable today. Despite himself, he felt an erection sprouting.

"What would... the *usual* be?"

He plucked a pack of Marlboro reds and a pack of condoms off the racks and put them on the counter. She batted the box of condoms off, sending them smacking onto the floor. Doug bent down to pick them up.

"What kind of a whore do you think I am?"

Doug's face flushed. He thought he was just trying to have fun with her.

"I just thought... maybe you used them all."

"Three times in one night?"

"Maybe you used them on a... project?"

Now he thought she was smirking. She curled a hand around the box of cigarettes. "Will you need my ID again today?"

"I don't think so." He'd memorized her birth date but thought it would be creepy to share that information.

"And what if I wanted to buy some alcohol? Like some Old Milwaukee or something?"

Now he thought she was definitely smirking.

"No. I wouldn't need to see it because I *know* you're not old enough."

Her smirk dropped away. Again, she stared into his eyes. Her pupils were huge. They almost blotted out the irises.

"Neither are you." It was nearly a hiss. "Besides, I wouldn't buy any anyway. It's sad to drink alone."

She *had* to be the one who made the totem. He almost asked her but was afraid of what her response might be.

"So, will this be all then? No paper?"

"Last night's murder isn't in the paper yet."

A tremor went through Doug's body.

"Murder?"

"You haven't heard about it yet?"

Doug shook his head. He almost told her about going out to look at the scene of the accident on Mountain Bottom Road, thinking that was probably something she would think was cool but he didn't because... Because why? Did he feel guilty he'd been with Mindy? Whitney wasn't his girlfriend. He didn't need to feel guilty about anything.

"I could tell you all about it."

"Who was it?"

"You'll find out."

The door to the office opened and Crank and Amber emerged. Amber was straightening her shirt and her shorts. Crank was smiling and either straightening or mussing what hair he had left. Doug, nervous that Crank and Whitney occupied the same space, hurriedly gave Whitney the total. She pulled a crumpled five from the waistband of her gypsy skirt. She stared straight down. Crank and Amber continued to the counter.

"Whitney Smith!" Crank bellowed. He seemed super high.

"Yep. That's my name." She took the cigarettes and the change and turned toward the front door.

"What's it been? Like four years? What the hell happened to you?"

"Stuff."

Crank's smile dropped away once he realized they had now run out of appropriate conversation. Trying to recover, he said, "This is Amber. Amber, Whitney."

"Hi Amber. Are you twelve?"

"She's *thirteen*," Crank said. "What kind of sicko do you think I am?"

"Okay. I have to go."

"Need a ride or anything?"

Doug's face flushed again as he realized Crank *would* have sex with Whitney if given the chance. And not because he was attracted to her but because he would see this shy, slightly unstable girl as some kind of conquest.

"Are you running a rickshaw service these days?"

Doug laughed, forcefully and loudly. All three of them turned to stare at him.

"I have to go," Whitney said. She held up the pack of cigarettes. "I've got smoking to do."

"Nice seein ya. You should come to our show on Friday. We're playin at the Ark Sakura..."

Whitney had already walked out the door.

Doug, in an attempt to keep Crank around until Whitney was far away, smiled and said, "The Ark Sakura, huh?"

Fifteen

Mindy said she needed gas before they left. Doug offered to pump. Mindy fed the company credit card into the machine. She wore the helmet with the visor flipped up, a skin tight black shirt and very short khaki shorts. Doug closed his mouth and looked away. Wiped the back of his hand against his chin to make sure he wasn't drooling. It was still light out, the air filled with all those early summer smells. It was times like this Doug wished he had a girlfriend. A beautiful summer day of his eighteenth year. It seemed like a waste to spend it alone. Although, technically, he guessed, he wasn't really alone. He was with Mindy. Then he would be alone. Or with Crank. Dang. He'd almost forgotten about going to Crank's house. Crank had said there was something he wanted to talk to him about. It could be anything. Crank was getting weird. Scary weird.

The pump kicked off.

Mindy stared at him. The helmet made her look like she was from the future or another planet.

Doug looked at the pump. He'd never pumped gas before, but he'd made it this far. He nervously pulled the handle from the car and gave it a couple of shakes.

"Aw, c'mon, don't you pump gas for your mom?"

Doug positioned the handle back on the pump.

"She never really asks," he said. "She'd probably only think I was doing it because I wanted something anyway."

"Wanna start driving?"

"Sure."

Doug sat behind the wheel.

"Soon we'll have to tackle the highway," Mindy said.

"That'll be pretty exciting."

"Hopefully not too exciting."

Doug started the car. "Do you mind dropping me off at a friend's house, instead of mine? When we're finished?"

"Is it too far away?"

"No, it's closer than home."

"Sure. You're eighteen. I'll drop you off wherever you tell me. Besides, you're driving. You go where you want."

How bout taking me home with you then? Doug thought.

Doug pulled out onto the road. As usual, there wasn't any traffic.

"So I know you go to church and stuff but what else do you do for fun?"

"Not a lot really. I like to play video games." He didn't want to tell her which one.

"Which ones?"

"Oh, all kinds..."

"That sounds lonely. Anything else?"

Doug thought of anything that could help him redeem himself. "Sometimes I like to drink. With Crank. The friend I was telling you about? That's where you're dropping me." He more or less blurted this out and then immediately thought he'd said the wrong thing. After all, if Mindy were devoted to the Church, she wouldn't want to think he drank for fun. Which was hyperbole at best and a lie at worst.

"Sounds like fun."

"What else is there to do?" Jesus, that sounded like something

Crank would say.

He turned the car off the state route.

"I'm glad you mentioned that. You know how so many people in the Church are. No this. No that. But they're old. They don't understand that younger people are more liberal and to tell them that everything is bad is just going to end up driving them away."

"Definitely."

"So, anyway, me and some friends are having a get together on Friday night."

"Friday?"

"Yeah. Everybody should be there by ten or eleven. You should come. I can give you directions and everything."

His heart leaped around in his chest and felt like it pushed blood forcefully through all of his limbs. It made him think he might blow up. He couldn't believe this was happening.

"That sounds great." His voice sounded weird. His throat felt constricted. His face was probably red. He hoped he didn't run them off the road.

"Just you, though, okay? It's not at my house and I wouldn't really feel comfortable extending the invitation to people I don't really know."

"Yeah, sure. No problem." He wondered if that meant no Crank or no girlfriend. But she knew he didn't have a girlfriend. No Crank. Either way it was fine with him. Crank. What day was Crank's show? It didn't matter. He'd seen Crank and his "band" play plenty of times. They'd probably still be practicing when he got there.

He drove deeper into the countryside, feeling really happy.

Sixteen

Doug got out of the car and Mindy told him she would see him Monday around five. Doug wanted to tell her that was too long to wait. He wanted her to say she would see him every day for the rest of their lives. She took off the helmet and tossed it into the back seat. Doug forced himself to look away as she sat behind the wheel and closed the door. He began walking over to where Chainsaw Enema was set up.

They didn't really have an indoor practice space so they just ran extension cords out from Crank's trailer. Amber was there, dancing around to the wild dissonance shooting from the amplifiers. Crank played his battered electric guitar furiously and without any recognizable chords or notes. The drummer, who went by the name Patrick Crayze, had his drum kit set up backward so he faced the trailer and away from the band. The keyboardist, Lurk, had passed out or something. The keyboard was off the stand but still turned on. Lurk's head rested on random keys providing a constant and eerie wash of sound. None of the band members wore shirts. Stupid tattoos were as ubiquitous as empty beer cans. Crank's mom held a hose and stood watering the side of the trailer. Doug felt like he had stumbled into recreation time at a mental institution.

As Doug drew closer, Crank stopped abusing his guitar. Patrick Crayze stopped drumming as soon as the guitar stopped. He reached to his right, grabbed a tall can of beer, and began chugging it. Crank moved over to Lurk and nudged his head off the keyboard. Amber continued dancing.

"You made it," Crank said.

"You said there was something you wanted to talk about."

Crank held a silencing finger over his lips. "Was that your driving coach?"

"Yeah."

"Fuckin hot."

"I guess so. We might be going out."

"No way."

"She invited me to a party she's having on Friday."

"Friday? That's the show!"

"I might have to miss it."

"I don't blame you. For a piece of that?"

"She didn't invite me over for intercourse. It's just a get together she's having at a friend's house."

Crank laughed. "They'll probably all pull their pussies out and shit."

Why would he say something like that?

Crank playfully punched him on the shoulder. "Trust me. Girls like that love to fuck. Know why? Cause they have awesome bodies. They know they're not going to look like that forever so they have to show it off as much as they can. I think Amber over there's already fucked every guy in the high school."

"High school?"

"Middle school. Whatever. Don't know what grade she's in."

Patrick Crayze crunched the beer can, tossed it off into the yard, hunched over and vomited. He woozily stood up.

"Hey!" he called like he was really far away even though it was only a few feet.

"What!" Crank barked at him.

"You got any more of those pills?"

Crank's mom turned the hose on Patrick and began watering him with a blank expression.

"They're in my drawer. Don't touch the weed." Crank scratched at the hair that was still taped to his arm.

Amber followed Patrick into the house. Crank's mom said she was going to the store and began walking toward the gravel road.

"By store she means bar," Crank said.

"She goes on foot?"

"Probably left her car there or somebody brought her home last night."

The thought of anyone bringing Crank's mom home gave Doug hives.

"Let's grab some chairs."

Doug followed Crank around the trailer. By chairs Crank meant industrial spools that had once contained wiring or something. They looked like they belonged on a pirate ship.

"What's up?" Doug asked.

"Freaky things."

Doug heard something he thought was a dog and realized it was Amber inside the trailer.

"Like what kind of freaky things?"

"Like, I don't know, *satanic* kinds of freaky things."

"You'll have to be more specific."

Crank told him about what had happened at Chloe's yesterday. In the interim, Amber had stopped barking. Now he was pretty sure she and Patrick were yelling at each other. Or the TV was up really loud. It was hot. Now that it was getting near dark, the humidity was alive. Doug wished he could pull his shirt off too. But he could never do that.

"So you think you saw the devil?" he asked.

"I'm pretty sure, yeah."

"And it was some frat guy named Daniel?"

"Yeah. That's right."

"And you're sure you weren't hallucinating?"

"That's where I don't really know. I talked to Chloe afterwards and she seemed fine except that this guy had totally roped her in. Which isn't really like her and it made me scared, man."

"But you don't even believe in God."

"It makes a lot more sense to believe in Satan, if you think about it. There's a lot more evil than good in the world."

"There's a lot of wickedness. But if you strip away the wickedness, I think you'd find that most people are good."

"I don't know, man. Most people I know just want to get high and fuck. Is that good or evil?"

"That is wickedness. So many problems arise from those things. Most of the conflicts you have... the acts themselves may not be wicked, but the aftermath can be. It's only evil if you do something with the intention of hurting someone."

"Why can't I be more like you, Doug?"

This shocked Doug.

"I mean, do you really believe in all that stuff? God and Satan? Heaven and Hell?"

"It's all in the Bible. It's what Pastor Larsta talks about every Sunday and Wednesday. Are you interested in going with me sometime? Tomorrow maybe?"

"Nah. I can't go tomorrow. It's too early. Maybe Wednesday though."

Doug paused and looked at the ground. Processing.

"What?" Crank said. "You don't want me around any of your churchy friends?"

"It's not that. You're my best friend. You know I'd love it if you came to church with me. But, if you come, I want you to be serious about it. Pay attention. No mocking. Don't show up drunk or high. Come with an open mind."

"I always come with an open mind." He smiled and playfully tapped Doug on the shoulder.

The door to the trailer slammed shut. Amber came barreling

around the corner. It looked like she had vomit on her shirt. She *smelled* like vomit.

"Your friend is an *asshole*!"

"So?" Crank said.

"Fuck you." She spit at him and then stamped off toward the road. Lost another one, Doug thought. This doesn't seem to be any place for women.

"Shit. I need to get drunk. Want one?"

Doug thought about it. Crank had agreed to come to church with him. It seemed like he should celebrate this miracle. He thought about what Mindy said about how it was natural for younger people to be more liberal and it didn't make them any less religious. And she was a member of the Tabernacle. Practically a nun. One of the chosen. He didn't want to stop thinking about Mindy. "Sure," he said.

Darkness came slowly. Patrick Crayze loaded Lurk up into a primer black car. Crank started a fire even though it was so hot out the extra heat just seemed to add a layer of misery. They sat around the fire, drank beers, and talked and laughed just like they used to. Doug stopped lamenting or wondering after the fact they had drifted so far apart ideologically while remaining so geographically close. Before the extreme drunkenness set in, Doug was having a very good time. Then he found it impossible to think or hold his eyes open. He was put into a car and taken home and walked up to his room.

As he lay in the darkness, the room spinning around him, he thought he heard howling and growling and possibly chanting. He dreamed of fire.

Seventeen

There was a knock at the door.

The house was so small, Amanda Winthrop only had to walk a few steps to reach it. People had been stopping by to drop all kinds of things off the last few days. Usually food. Mostly cakes and really fattening things. She left most of them sitting on the counter. Maybe people would eat them at the post-funeral gorge fest. The funeral was tomorrow afternoon. She'd be happier when it was all over.

She opened the door.

A familiar face stared back at her. It was familiar but out of context. When it finally hit her who the striking man was, her knees nearly buckled.

"Amanda Winthrop?" He held out a bouquet of roses.

It was Lawrence Kansas, star of *Johnny Got His Gun: The Series*. It was a dreadful television show consisting of a man, played by Lawrence Kansas, lying in bed and hysterically shouting as they removed parts of his body, alternating with nostalgic flashbacks and surreal dream sequences. She didn't really like the show but she enjoyed watching Kansas. He looked different standing up. He looked different with arms and legs.

"Lawrence Kansas? Why would you be here?"

"I heard you were going through a rough patch."

"Well, yes, my husband died but this is... quite a surprise."

She took the flowers and, for just a moment, thought she saw his blue irises turn the color of fire.

"I'd better get some water for these."

"May I come in?"

Behind him, the insects chirped. The thick air seemed filled with perfume.

"Of course."

She turned and crossed the small room into the kitchen. She filled a glass with cold water, tore the rubberbanded cellophane from the roses, and put them in the glass. Kansas's appearance was quite a mystery. She couldn't wait to get to the bottom of it.

When she re-entered the living room, Kansas stood in the middle of it. He was naked. He held his penis with his right hand, stroking it slowly.

"Mr. Kansas! My mother's asleep in the other room. She's very sick. My husband just died."

He waved her complaints away. "I'm aware of all these things. It sounds like this," he brandished his member at her, "is something you could really use."

She knew there wasn't a need to argue with him. Her sex had begun to moisten as soon as she saw him standing there. She hadn't had sex with Perry in six months. Since they'd been married, she'd had sex with three other guys. Just drunken one night stands but still... she didn't think the grieving widow routine was any reason to pass on this opportunity.

She crossed the room and kneeled at the altar of his cock. She had never been this worked up before. It was nearly otherworldly. She took him into her mouth. He removed her clothes savagely. She apologized for being unbathed and stubbly. He went down on her anyway, his tongue snaking her insides, disappearing up her asshole. Things became disconnected and fragmented. When he entered her, she thought she was going to break open. They moved into as many positions as possible, staying in one until her muscles quivered. It seemed to go on and on until the house was finally dark. Eventually she had come so many times her vagina had gone dry. Then he pulled out and finished in her mouth, fingertips clamped on her nipples. His come tasted like blood and sulfur.

He held her and whispered strange things in her ear. They moved into her mother's room. He asked Amanda if she thought the old lady wanted it too. She didn't know how to respond. Things were dark and hazy. The room swirled around her. He crawled up on the bed, between her mother's legs. Amanda could still taste him at the back of her throat. She spread his ass and began licking while he pumped away at her mother.

She blacked out.

Came to at her mother's bedside. Kansas had opened up her arm and was drinking the blood. He offered the arm to Amanda. She accepted. Drank. Vomited. Drank some more. Told herself it was like drinking wine.

Then, in deep night, she had a vision of Lawrence Kansas, flush with sex and her mother's blood, dancing around the house, eating all the condolence food, sprouting horns and hooves and a tail, entertaining three more women, girls who couldn't have been far from their teenage years.

And then Amanda had staggered outside, naked and sore but feeling so alive. She collapsed on the dewy grass and remained there until Kansas came to retrieve her and place her in the bed next to her now dead mother.

Amanda woke up the next morning and screamed until she realized her life was now perfect. She couldn't help but feel like she owed somebody for that.

Sunday, June 15th

Eighteen

Later that morning, Amanda awoke again. This time to the ringing of the phone. She was in her mother's bed, which was odd. It triggered some memory but the ringing of the phone kept her from dwelling on it. Her mother wasn't in the bed. The old woman was basically immobile and the first tendril of panic ran down Amanda's spine.

Standing in the living room, she picked up the phone, already scouting the house for her mother.

"Hello?"

"Ms. Winthrop?"

"Yes?"

"You've undoubtedly noticed the absence of your mother."

"Yes."

Her mother was dead. She knew this without asking. She remembered waking up next to the corpse. But she had been so elated she had gone back to sleep.

"I want you to know that it's being taken care of."

"Who is this? What's being taken care of?"

Now Amanda stood in her bedroom, inspecting her naked body in the full-length mirror. Scratches and bruises and blood everywhere.

"I'm sorry. This is Bob Beals from Beals Funeral Home. I was calling to let you know that we have your mother here. The arrangements have all been taken care of."

"Who...? "

"A Mr. Lawrence Kansas. You keep some very high class company."

Amanda's head was spinning. She tried to make sense of anything. She was sore all over: her rear, her vagina, her jaws, arms, legs, stomach. Even her tongue was sore.

"I was simply wondering if you would like to combine her funeral with Perry's."

It all seemed so unconventional. Who had called them? When had they come to retrieve the body?

"I'm well aware of how much turmoil a funeral can cause. I thought maybe this would be easier than turning around and having another funeral for a loved one in two days."

She didn't know what to say. She quickly scanned her mind and tried to think of people to invite. She couldn't think of anyone she hadn't already notified regarding Perry's death.

"That's... fine. Thank you, Mr. Beals."

"Please, call me Bob. The schedule will remain the same so you have nothing to worry about. As I mentioned before. Everything's been taken care of."

"I... I don't know what to say."

"You don't have to say anything."

So she didn't say anything. Beals continued to breathe on the other end of the line.

"Thanks again, Mr... Bob. I'll see you at the funeral."

"Certainly, Ms. Winthrop and, I was wondering, since you're single and free of responsibility now, perhaps you'd like to go to dinner some time?"

Amanda's brow creased. That didn't seem like an appropriate question. She couldn't even recall what Bob Beals looked like, even though she knew she'd seen him before. But he was being very nice and, as she slumped down on the cool lid of the toilet, she had a vision of him over top of her, clutching her legs beneath the knees and shoving them up over her head, spreading her apart, ramming into her, filling her.

"Sure... Bob."

"Great. I've heard you're quite the piece."

She was already touching herself, sliding fingers into her sore vagina.

"Oh," she breathed into the phone. "I am. You have no idea."

Bob laughed lecherously. "I'll see you at the services then."

"Mmmm." Amanda clicked the phone off and brought herself to a climax.

Nineteen

Doug's bed rocked back against the wall. His stomach lurched. He opened his eyes and the ceiling spun in the distance.

His bed rocked again.

His room smelled like vomit and alcohol. He was damp with sweat. The alcohol fumes seemed to be coming from his pores.

"Wake up!"

His bed rocked again.

Jeez. What had he done last night? He still felt drunk. He had drunk mouth. His stomach heaved again. He started to get out of bed so he could dash for the bathroom until he saw the soiled trash can sitting next to the bed. Someone had taken care of him. He vomited into the trash can.

The bed-kicker moved in front of him.

"You should be ashamed of yourself," he said.

It was Deacon Pork, the Sunday school teacher. Why was Deacon Pork here in his bedroom?

Doug looked at his clock. There were two sets of numbers but they seemed to agree that it was 10:20.

He'd missed church. Missed church because he was hung over.

Deacon Pork was hunched over in front of him, only a few

inches from his face. He wore a navy blue wrestling singlet. Pork was shaped like a triangle. His head was like an enormous potato. A potato on top of a triangle. His mouth was an intense line under a well-clipped black mustache.

"You had your mother in tears, boy."

Doug swung his legs off the bed and sat with his sweaty head clasped between his hands.

"I'm sorry," he said.

"You better believe it. You're the sorriest Christian I've ever seen. Your poor mother. Don't you know alcohol is just Satan's lubrication?"

"I'm sorry."

Pork slapped him.

"I'm really thirsty."

"A small price to pay. Imagine how I felt when I entered the Sunday school room and I was the only one there."

"Where was Lankmeyer?" Jim Lankmeyer was always there. Jim never missed a day. He went to seminary school in Cincinnati. Doug figured it was only a matter of time before Jim was the pastor of his own church.

"Jim Lankmeyer is no longer with us. Another one of the Devil's victims."

This could have meant any number of things.

"He's..."

"Jim Lankmeyer's dead, boy."

"I'm so sorry."

Doug thought about the death Whitney had mentioned. The one that wasn't in the paper yesterday morning.

Until Pork slapped him again.

"He was running around with that Coleman girl. They found him in the woods. His genitals were out. Apparently it was some kind of sex game. The Tabernacle is disciplining her. I'm here to discipline you."

"I'm really thirsty. Thirsty and sorry."

"Mouth's burned up with the fires of hell."

Doug vomited again. His life was over. If he ever wanted to leave the house again he would have to move out.

"Your poor mother sent me over here to discipline you and I wondered how I should go about it. There's nothing I can say to you when you have that poison rattling around in your soul. That poison's saying, 'Satan is good.' That poison's saying, 'Satan is fun.'" Now he moved around the room like he was preaching a sermon. Sometimes he filled in for Pastor Larsta and usually preached one evening of their week long revivals. "So I remembered when I was in college and I used to wrestle the Devil every weekend. You know I never lost? Some folks say you can't beat the Devil, but I beat him every time and that victory was glorious. That victory was power and glory. Glory glory. That victory has lasted every day of my life. When my peers and sometimes even my loved ones would try to feed me to the fires of sin, I was able to resist. I was able to get them to submit. When the jezebels and the harlots of the world would try to get me to lay in sin with them, I was able to administer a stranglehold. When the demons would try to grapple my soul away, I was able to put them in a full-nelson and squeeze my arms around their shoulders. Glory glory. Understand what I'm trying to tell you, boy?"

Doug really didn't.

Pork slapped him again.

"I've come to defeat your demons."

He ripped Doug off the bed, took him to the floor, and slapped a half-nelson on him.

"You gotta fight back! You gotta fight the demons!"

Doug was hot and woozy. He didn't know how long he spent fighting the demons. Both he and Pork worked up a great sweat. They struggled around the room, Pork panting in his ear and yelling Bible scriptures at him, peppered with the occasional, "Glory glory". Finally, when he was unable to move any more, Pork said, "Now go get in the shower and wash that sin off a ya.

And just think, the next time you feel like submitting, you could spiral into addiction. You could give up your virginity. You could become a gay. And if you lose that innocence, our church will have no use for you. And then you'll have nothing. Nothing but demons."

Doug waited until he was gone and then took a shower. He didn't have to work today so he lay in bed and waited for his mother. He wanted to play *Redemption* but he was too tired. He decided that, the next time he played, he was going to fuck anything he could get his virtual hands on.

But he'd never play *Redemption* again.

Twenty

Amanda had never been to the Church for anything other than a funeral. She didn't really know what to expect. For a few years as a child her parents had dragged her to a Baptist church. She remembered the services as loud, volatile things full of fire and brimstone and damnation. She guessed it put her off religion for good. Well, maybe not for good. Not if she was here now. She couldn't dismiss it as mere convenience. It would have been far more convenient to stay home and welcome any out-of-town guests who happened to show up early or ready the house for the post-funeral reminiscences and feast. But, well, she had felt compelled. Maybe that's what people meant when they described themselves as being filled with the Holy Spirit.

Once in the Church, she was greeted warmly. Hands were shaken. Hugs were received. She sat near the back, an out of place smile plastered across her face. She felt welcome here. She didn't know many members of the congregation. The congregation was mostly made of women. The only men she saw were the ushers and, of course, Pastor Larsta.

People slowly took their seats. The Church filled with politely hushed coughs, muffled conversation, and the flipping of onionskin Bible pages. Several times she caught people looking at her. They would smile or flip a quick consoling wave in her direction.

Pastor Larsta moved behind the podium and began speaking. His "sermon" was brief and bizarre. Amanda didn't know what to think. Maybe this was how he kept his congregation from getting bored.

He raised both arms out from his body and began speaking, keeping his arms outstretched. His smile was giant and maniacal, his cheeks rosy and, even from where she sat, Amanda could see how his eyes sparkled. Here, she knew, was a man truly filled with the same spirit she was. Here was a man in love with the Lord.

"Happy Sunday, boys and girls, mostly girls!" He sounded like a public access clown. Amanda almost giggled. It felt good. He lowered his arms and started flapping his hands around his head. "We've had some tragedies this week." Still in that big clown voice. "Some people died! Were maybe even *killed*! But the police will sort that out! We're here on God's business!"

He pumped his right fist furiously into the perfumed air.

"God's business!" he yelled.

He pumped his fist again and the congregation chanted along with him: "God's business!"

Then they too were pumping their fists. Amanda felt the spirit surge through her, even more powerfully now. She pumped her fist in the air and chanted, "God's business!" along with the rest of them. She felt flush. She felt a familiar tingling in her lower stomach and wondered if it would be wrong to have an orgasm in church.

Larsta ended the chant with a coughing fit. It turned his face even redder.

"But, oh sisters and brothers, mostly sisters, the month marches on! The days march on. The days have hours and minutes!"

He hopped up and down, grabbed a cup of water, took a gulp and thew it off to the side like a marathon runner. He ran to the back pew and then back up to the pulpit where he stumbled and nearly fell.

"But we'll stop time in the eyes of the Lord! We'll have our own paradise right here because that's what God wants. God wants us all to be happy! Happy! Happy! Happy!"

Again he pumped his fist. Again the congregation joined him.

"Because we all know that Satan stalks these mountains and he comes in the form of the pious. So we must lure him to us. We must cast a web, a Jesus web, and ensnare him." He held his hands splayed before him.

"But enough of my blather... Let's have some communion and then some fellowship. That's really what Jesus is all about: communing and fellowshipping. Woo! Glory glory!"

The ushers began going down the rows and handing out bottles of wine and wafers of the host. The women would pop the host and take slugs of the wine. People had begun talking animatedly.

"And I'd like to welcome our latest member to the congregation: Ms. Amanda Winthrop. After suffering the tragic losses of her husband and mother, Amanda now joins you in your freedom!"

Now Amanda couldn't help but smile even more broadly. A laugh even escaped her lips. She couldn't remember the last time she had laughed at anything other than the television or her own misfortune.

"Come on up here!" Larsta shouted. Or did he say, "Get that ass up here!"? Amanda couldn't quite hear him. She still had that tingly feeling in her lower gut and the pastor had called her a member. Their latest member. She couldn't remember the last time she had felt this good.

She walked, nearly ran, to the front of the Church. Larsta had come down from behind the pulpit. He held his arms out. She fell into them. He wrapped his arms around her, his scent filling her nostrils. It reminded her of Lawrence Kansas and her blissful night came back to her. The pastor handed her a bottle of wine and placed the host on her tongue. She swallowed the host and washed it down with a slug of wine. Larsta turned her around to face the congregation and then pressed on her shoulders until she sat on the wooden altar. Written on the front of the altar, in blood red letters, was: FOR HE SO LOVED THE WORLD.

Larsta kneeled down in front of her. She took another slug from the bottle. Her head swam. She noticed all the blinds had been drawn and the lights dimmed. Larsta slid his hands up the outside of her legs, under her dress until his fingers were in the waistband of her panties. Some members of the congregation looked on but many of them appeared to be making out. Larsta slowly pulled her underwear down her legs. Then he lifted up her legs, placing them over his shoulders, and plunged his tongue into her. She gasped and came immediately. Many of the women were in the center aisle on their hands and knees, forming a line of mutual cunnilingus. The ushers were pounding into several of the women in the front row. The pastor stopped lapping at her, patted her vagina, and moved away. Then the first member of the congregation kneeled down in front of her. The woman unbuttoned the top of Amanda's dress and began playing with her nipples as she sucked on Amanda's clit. Amanda was lost in a realm of bliss. She didn't know how many people came to ply her vagina and anus with their tongues but, just when she thought that she wanted it to last forever, Larsta came back, turned her over until she was on her knees, elbows resting on the altar. He slid into her. He was very large. Larger even than Lawrence Kansas. It was painful at first. He fed her another host and continued to slide in and out of her. Eventually she was crying out in ecstasy. Then he stepped away and moved to her side, stroking himself. The next man took his place.

This continued until, finally, they laid her down on the altar. A few men emptied themselves into her mouth and she drank it down with glee. The rest of them showered her in their come, wetting her in droplets and ropes of heat. She wiped some semen out of her eyes and looked around. The congregation was all gathered around her, smiling and sweaty, empty and exhausted, but so happy and full of life.

Twenty-one

Doug woke up and looked at the ceiling. The room was very bright. It had to be some time in the afternoon. He didn't want to move his head to look at his clock. He still felt like garbage. Maybe Crank had put something in his beers. He remembered feeling really good while he was drinking. Maybe wrestling with Deacon Pork had made him feel bad. Strained his muscles or something. He turned his head to the right.

Whitney Smith stared down at him.

For a second, he thought maybe he was dreaming.

Once he realized it was actually her, his heart sped up. He didn't know if it was from excitement or fear.

"Whitney Smith."

"Doug Backus."

He waited for her to say something else. When she didn't he said, "What are you doing in my room?"

"Just looking around. I got bored. Sundays are always boring as fuck. Remember when things used to be closed on Sundays? Like they were enforcing boredom or something."

She sat down at the foot of his bed and crossed her legs, right over left. The right foot bounced a lot. She wasn't wearing any shoes. Her toe nails weren't painted. She pulled a cigarette from behind her left ear and lit it with a lighter she had been holding.

"You can't smoke in here," Doug said.

"Relax."

"If my mom finds out..."

"She's not here. There were like three funerals today. She'll probably be gone for a while. One of them's for that guy I was telling you about. The dumb ass who ran his car off the road? I bet they're all closed casket."

She took a drag off her cigarette and exhaled a plume of smoke. Doug coughed.

"Don't be one of those people."

"I don't like smoke. It's a gross, expensive habit."

"Then don't do it."

She flicked her ash on the floor and ground it in with her foot.

"You know another disgusting habit?" she said. "Drinking until you puke."

He took a breath and noticed, even with the cloud of cigarette smoke, that the puke smell was gone from his room. He looked beside his bed.

"I took care of it," Whitney said.

"Thanks." He didn't like the thought of her being around his vomit-filled trash can.

"I mean I took care of all of it."

"Did you bring me home last night?"

She shrugged.

"Why?"

"It was something to do. I drove over to Crank's because I figured someone would be there. You were, but neither of you was conscious. Luckily, you were able to walk to the car. I had to threaten you with your mom."

"That's so embarrassing."

"It happens. I'm starting to realize being embarrassed is what it means to be an adult."

Doug closed his eyes. "What *is* my mom going to say?"

"If you're lucky, she'll just think you were sick. Or *pretend* to just think you're sick. You probably smelled like a keg so she'd have to be an idiot not to know you were hungover. But, since you've been such a good little boy, she might let you get away with it this one time. Besides, how can she really punish you? You're eighteen. All you do is go to work and what, play video games or something? And you *like* to go to church, which is punishment for most people. Even the people who go all the time feel like they have to atone for something. So maybe you'll get a stern talking to or yelling at or something."

"I hope. I'm pretty sure she knows I was hungover. But maybe I've already been disciplined.

"Have you ever had sex?"

"What kind of question is that?"

"You just... when I asked for the condoms the other day, you turned so red. And you're so religious and everything..." She took a final drag from her cigarette. "So, are you... a virgin, I mean?"

"Yes. Of course I am. Premarital sex is a sin."

She laughed.

"Have you?" he asked.

"Not with a boy."

"Then you're technically a virgin, too."

"I don't know about that. End result's the same thing."

She held the smoldering butt in her fingertips. She stood up and looked down at him. "You should come by my house tomorrow."

"I could probably come tonight."

"Tonight I've got things. Tomorrow would be better."

"I've gotta go to work in the morning. Then I have a driving lesson." Driving lesson. Mindy. Mindy had asked him to a party.

"Well, I'm up late. Come after all that, if you can."

"I'll see."

"Do that."

She left the room in a swirling cloud of smoke, not bothering to shut the door behind her.

Twenty-two

The rest of Amanda's day passed in a blissful haze. There was the church service followed by a period of murkiness and then she found herself standing at the front of the Church next to Jim Lankmeyer's mother, Marcy, and staring at tearful faces and giving out hugs and receiving hugs. A lot of friends and relatives following their scripts.

"So sorry for your loss..."

"If you need anything..."

"Can't imagine what you must be going through..."

Amanda concentrated to affix a dour, sorrowful look on her face when what she wanted to do was smile and laugh, shake her friends' and family members' hands, clap them on the back and say, "It's all right. I'm already over it. I feel great. My mother had been dying for years, was actually dead on the day my father died, and Perry, well, Perry was a cheating, lying, greedy son of a whore."

Then there was more standing as the whole grim, black procession moved to the cemetery, followed by the loose procession (the flags removed from the cars) back to her house. The house was immaculate. The spread had been laid out. Someone must have done this. Amanda had no recollection of it.

Later in the afternoon, Pastor Larsta came by with a vanload of flowers, laying them out all over the house, wherever there was room. After the last person had left, Amanda was alone with the flowers. She opened all the blinds in the house and let the late afternoon sunlight pour in. She lay down in the middle of the living room floor and laughed uncontrollably. She imagined Lawrence Kansas was there, peeling off her clothes, filling her up, bringing her to shuddering climax after shuddering climax.

When the last of the day's light left, she took the flowers outside, over the course of several trips, and set fire to them. She got drunk on wine and danced around the fire, ripped off her clothes, felt the moonlight on her body. Eventually, she was joined by a group of women, most of them probably ten years younger than she was. They were led by a man. The man made Amanda think of a goat. He made her think of the Devil. She wanted to touch his curly hair to see if she'd feel horns.

The man put his fingers to her lips, peremptorily staunching any protests. He told her she was coming with them. He told her she was going to be a witness.

Witness, Amanda thought.

First a member, then a witness.

The word—maybe it was even more than a word, maybe it was a title—made her feel powerful.

She piled into the van with them. The goat man wrapped a heavy black blindfold around her head.

"How can I be a witness if I can't see?" Amanda asked.

The goat man laughed.

The girls laughed.

Amanda laughed, too.

Twenty-three

Doug stayed in his bed most of the day. He went downstairs twice to get something to eat and drink. Neither time did it do anything to quench his amazing thirst or nourish his amazing hunger. The first time he went downstairs was in the early afternoon. His mother had come back between the regular church service and the funerals. She stared at the television and laughed like an idiot. She didn't notice him. The second time she sat in a chair facing the fireplace, where his father's gleaming silver cross-shaped urn rested on the mantle. The low sun beamed in through the window and caught the cross in an interesting way, reflecting off it and onto his mother's face. Beatific was a word Doug had heard before and he thought that described the way she looked even if he didn't know the exact meaning of it. Again, she didn't notice him.

On his way back through the living room, on the other side of the sunlight, looking at the darker side of her face, he just thought she looked old. Ancient. Too old to be anybody's mother. He grabbed the phone, retreated to his room, and called Crank. Either Crank wasn't home or he wasn't answering. Maybe he was at the station. He usually knew Crank's schedule but his brain was in a fog and he couldn't think of it right now. It took a second just to jog the number of America Pantry from his head. The phone rang a couple of times and Patel said, "America Pantry."

Doug hung up.

A second later, the phone rang. The America Pantry number popped up on the caller ID screen. Maybe Crank *was* there.

"Hello," Doug said.

"I know who this is," Patel said. "Why you think I pay for caller ID? To keep punks like you from calling. Why you call anyway? Call and hang up."

"I was just calling to see if Crank was there."

"Crank's not here. If he was here, he would have answered the phone. Why would I pay him to be here if I'm here?"

"I'm not feeling well." Doug didn't know what else to say.

"I think you are sick with rudeness. I think this whole town is sick with rudeness. This morning I came in and find a bag of hair on the counter. Was this your bag of hair?"

Bag of hair? "Mr. Patel, I don't know what you're talking about. I'm not feeling well at all. I need to get off the phone so I can go throw up."

"See. That is a very rude thing to say. What do you punks say? Too much information. Rude. You be here tomorrow?"

"Ten o'clock."

"Nine."

"Nine?"

"You call and hang up without saying nothing. Nine o'clock."

"I'll try."

"You will."

Doug gagged into the phone even though his nausea was long over, and clicked the OFF button. He opened his bedroom door, threw the phone down the stairs, and shouted, "I gotta be at work at nine tomorrow!"

He didn't listen for his mother's response. He turned off his lights, crawled into bed, pulled the sheet up over his head and thought about Whitney, Mindy, and masturbation. Then he fell asleep.

Twenty-four

When they finally removed the blindfold, Amanda stood in front of a small structure in the middle of the woods. She had no idea where she was. The structure looked like a small church. It had a cross jutting up off the roof. Had she not vaguely recollected what happened at the Church that morning, she would have been confused. Her stomach fluttered at the prospect of more group sex. She was sore and didn't know if she could physically take any more but there was longing deep inside her and she knew, if offered, she wouldn't refuse.

She followed the goat man and the three girls inside.

The girls went around the interior and lit candles as if they knew where they were by memory. Amanda didn't know what she was supposed to do.

The goat man was huge. His fleshy penis dangled between his legs and he made no attempt to cover it.

"How did you like the services this morning?" he asked.

"They were *great*." Amanda's voice sounded dreamy and distant, even to herself. "Were you there?" She thought about saying she didn't see anybody who looked like the Devil or a giant goat but thought that might sound like a smartass thing to say.

"I'm everywhere, child." He held out his hand and stroked a claw under her chin.

"Who are you? I've never seen you anywhere."

"You've seen me plenty of times. Who I am is not important. I am one of many. I have another question for you." He moved closer to her and his penis had stiffened somewhat. She felt it bumping into her stomach.

"Okay."

"How would you like for every moment of every day to be just like what you experienced in the Church today?"

"I think that would be like... like..."

"Heaven on earth?"

"Exactly."

"Soon. Soon, child, and I'm glad you want to be part of it. You *do* want to be part of it, don't you?"

"Oh, more than anything."

There was a knock on the door. "Angie!" the goat man called. "Please answer the door."

Angie flicked out a match and quickly walked to the door. Before opening it, she asked, "Who is it?"

"Baal's Goats on Demand."

She smiled and opened the door. A small goat entered the room.

"Just need you to sign this," the delivery man said.

Angie signed the clipboard.

"Enjoy." The man turned to leave.

The goat man was gripping himself with his right hand. "Mindy! Ready the knife!"

Mindy brought over a large knife. She had a savage gleam in her eye. Amanda empathized with it. She probably had the same gleam. She wanted them to fall upon the harmless little goat, slash its throat, throw its blood around and roll in it. The three girls seemed fresh and nubile. She wanted to see them without any clothes. She wanted to spread them open. Taste them. Put her fingers on them and in them. She wanted the goat man's cock to fill her throat. She wanted him to pound her ass. She was already moist and practically moaning.

"Kristen! Come and hold the goat! Mindy, hand the knife to our guest."

Mindy wrapped her hand around the blade and offered the haft to Amanda. She had a tight grip on it. Amanda tugged gently but the knife didn't come out of Mindy's hand. "Go ahead," Mindy said. "Take it."

Amanda yanked on the knife. Mindy made a fist with her hand and let the blood drip onto the back of the goat. She lifted up her skirt and smeared blood on her crotch. She dropped to the floor in front of the goat and spread her legs. The goat began lapping at the blood between her legs. Mindy made wild barking sounds, her body frantically quivering.

"Do it now!" the goat man shouted.

Amanda straddled the back of the goat, held the knife against its throat and slashed. Blood drenched Mindy. She threw off her clothes and rolled around in it. Amanda threw off her clothes as well. Angie was on her knees in front of the goat man, taking his huge cock deep into her mouth. Kristen stood off in a corner, the candlelight turning her blond hair orange, writhing to the sounds of moaning and the dying sound of the goat's hooves on the floor. Watching her, Amanda began to feel predatory. She moved toward the girl. She lifted up her dress to touch herself as she watched Kristen dance and, once again, the scene from that morning's church service came back to her. She continued moving toward her. Reaching her, she stopped her dancing and got down on her knees in front of her while Kristen ground against her face.

She didn't know how long this continued. There were chants and screams of pleasure. Something that might have been a prayer. The last thing she remembered was having her face buried in Kristen's vagina while the goat man pounded into her ass. Mindy was writhing in the goat, reduced to a pile of fur and offal. The goat man raked a savage hand across the back of Amanda's neck, clearing away the hair. As he made his final thrusts, he took a bite from the back of her neck. She cried out with pain but, at the same time, she liked it. She wanted more. She never wanted to leave.

She woke up in her room the next morning. The blinds and curtains were drawn. She didn't want to open them. She didn't want to leave the house. She went back to bed and waited for nightfall.

Monday, June 16th

Twenty-five

It was nine-oh-four and Doug stood behind the counter, staring glassy-eyed at the trashed store in front of him. It was like everyone in Clover had gone feral. Nothing unusual, he knew. The weekends were always bad. He imagined he was the only one who did anything. Patel was the owner and, therefore, too good to clean up. And then there was Crank. Doug knew what it was like when Crank was there by himself. It was a hangout and lived up to its name because, for Crank and his friends, it was a pantry. Doug wondered why Patel had never caught on that their inventory was way off. Maybe it didn't matter. Maybe Patel was only running this place to lose money. Doug knew he would end up cleaning the store and straightening the shelves but he didn't think he could do it right now. Even though he had slept most of yesterday, he still felt tired. Weighed down. Maybe he was getting sick.

Around ten, Deacon Pork came into the store, accompanied by a much smaller man wearing a black and white striped referee shirt. Pork wore the wrestling singlet he had on yesterday. Doug couldn't tell if it was the same one or not. Doug said hi but Pork just stared at him and maybe growled.

Pork walked down the pet food aisle, grabbed a fifty pound bag of dog food and slammed it onto the floor. Doug thought about stopping him but then assumed the Deacon was just trying to make some kind of point. Pork threw himself on the bag of dog food and the small man by his side crouched down and slammed his palm to the floor three times. Then he and Pork stood up together and he raised Pork's hand into the air.

The whole thing was silent and weird. Doug took a gulp of his Yoo-Hoo.

Pork then kicked the bag and nuggets of dog food went rolling all over the floor. It looked like Doug would be cleaning up sooner than he wanted to. Or he could just leave. It probably didn't really matter in the long run.

Pork and the referee came up to the counter. Pork said, "That's how you wrestle the demons," and the referee nodded. Pork reached his large hand out and grabbed Doug's Yoo-Hoo. He held it under his nose and took a whiff. Then he took a drink. Yoo-Hoo clung to the bottom of his mustache and Pork made no attempt to wipe it away. "I'll see you Wednesday," Pork said before he turned to leave.

"Definitely," Doug said.

He watched them exit the store. For the first time possibly, Wednesday would be the first day he dreaded going to church. It occurred to him he didn't really *have* to go. He was eighteen, after all. But his mom would freak. It seemed like the only thing he did to please her and, up until yesterday, he had liked going. Something had changed. He didn't know if it was Pork's actions, all the things Crank had said to him over the years, or if it was just something inside of him shifting around with the prospect of a driver's license and more freedom. He put the cap on his bottle of Yoo-Hoo and dropped it into the trash can. Then he went into the utility room and grabbed the broom and the dustpan-on-a-stick.

Around two a semi pulled up. The truck driver climbed down out of the cab and walked toward the store. He had a perplexed look on his face and kept glancing back at the truck. By the time the truck driver made it to the counter, he seemed angry and winded. Doug knew it couldn't be good. Through his experience, the truck drivers never really wanted to deal with what they had in their trucks and he knew the only thing causing this paroxysm of grief was some sort of huge shipment. But they usually received their large shipments on Monday and then the occasional small distributor through the week. This wasn't the normal trucking company. Doug stared at him while the man huffed and wheezed.

"Where you want all this stuff?"

"Um, we've got a loading dock in back. Most things come through there."

"Nah, I've delivered here before. You ain't got that much space."

"Okay."

The driver stared at him like he had a vagina on his forehead.

"So where you want it?"

"What is it?"

"Five thousand Duraflame logs."

"That has to be a mistake."

The driver slammed his metal clipboard down on the counter and pointed a black-rimmed fingernail.

"S'what the order says."

Doug looked at it but didn't really know what he was looking at.

"Let me call the owner," Doug said.

"I can't wait around all day."

"Just... one minute, okay?"

The driver stormed off back through the aisles. Doug grabbed the cordless phone and pressed the speed dial number for Patel, studying the invoice the entire time. The phone rang and rang. A name on the invoice jumped out at him and he hung up the phone. Patel's name wasn't on it. Stephen Tanas' was. Crank. Asshole. He thought about calling Crank to make sure *he* had ordered the Duraflames but knew it wouldn't do any good. If he actually answered his phone this early in the afternoon, he knew what he would say. Of course he had ordered the logs. In Crank's world, it didn't matter if anything made sense or not. It didn't matter that, if he actually wanted the logs for himself, it would cost many thousands of dollars.

The driver stood in the back of the store chugging a forty.

Doug flapped his hand at him to try and signal him back to the front. The driver capped the forty and put it back in the refrigerator.

Doug signed the invoice and slid it back to the driver, telling him they could start putting them in back and then finish putting them in the front.

Doug helped. It didn't take them nearly as long as he thought it would. Thankfully, they were in boxes. The only place in the front of the store not covered in merchandise was the window, so they stacked them floor to ceiling in front of that. When they were finished, the driver went back to the cooler to retrieve his forty, grabbed another one and said, holding them up above his shoulders, "Enjoy your Duraflames, fucker!" before walking out of the store.

Doug thought maybe the guy had some sort of personality disorder.

He picked up the phone to call Crank. He didn't know what his plans for the logs were but if they were there when Patel came in, he was going to throw a fit. While he was on the phone, Crank stormed in the front door. Lurk's truck was parked on the handicap ramp in front of the door, backed in. Lurk hung out the driver's side window and vomited.

"Hey, my fuckin Duraflames are here!" Crank shouted. Then said, "Who's callin?" He reached into the pockets of his black cargo shorts, pulled out the phone and said, "You're callin? Why are you callin me, Doug?"

"Because of those," Doug pointed to the wall of boxes in front of the windows. "You better get all of these out of here before Patel comes in in a couple of hours."

"No worries, bro!"
"Why do you need so many of them?"
"White trash pyrotechnics. For the show!"
Bad idea, Doug thought. Really bad idea.

Twenty-six

Three truckloads later, the front of the store was cleared of Duraflames. Doug helped Crank move all the ones from the stockroom out behind the dumpsters off the loading dock. Crank said he would come back and get the rest of them later. Since Patel never threw anything away, they figured they were safe.

By the time Patel showed up, the store was still trashed and Doug was sweaty and tired.

"Looks like pig barn," Patel said.

"We were real busy," Doug said.

"Always busy. Never make much money. Mystery."

"Maybe we need to start charging more." Doug didn't know what else to say.

The front of Patel's pants were swollen and he looked anxiously at his porn drawer. "Still here," he said.

"Just leaving." Doug clocked out and went to wait outside. Standing against the warm brick of the store and waiting for the Chariot Driving car to show up, he found himself fantasizing about Mindy. It was really hot out. He hoped she had downdressed appropriately. He shouldn't be having thoughts like that. She was as religious as he was and he was objectifying her. Not just objectifying *her* but tainting his brain with impure thoughts.

Finally, she pulled into the parking lot and got out from the driver's side. Doug found himself staring at her in a completely unsatisfied way. She wore something that was a cross between a druid's cloak and a nun's habit. She waved as she moved around to the passenger side. Until she was that close, Doug wasn't even sure it *was* Mindy. He slid into the driver's seat.

"That outfit's new," he said.

"Oh, this..." She reached into the backseat and grabbed her helmet. She slid the hood down to her shoulders. Her blond hair was done up in a severe bun. She had to unleash the knot of hair to get the helmet on. He waited for an explanation about the garb but didn't get one. With the helmet on, she could have been anyone. The cloak was so loose, he couldn't make any trace of her form, which was probably the point. He wondered if he was the cause of the change of dress. Maybe she had seen him gawking at her on one of their previous drives.

She casually told him places to turn and he followed her directions. They made small talk.

"Have any plans for this evening?" she asked.

"Not much. Hanging out with a friend."

"That Crank guy again?"

"No. He's busy getting ready for his show."

"Oh."

"It's a girl named Whitney Smith." Doug thought maybe that would make him seem like less of a loser.

"Oh, a girl. Your mom lets you hang around with girls?"

"She doesn't know. Besides, I'm hanging out with a girl right now."

"Well, that's different. I'm like a teacher. She knows you're safe with me."

Doug didn't like to hear that. That made it seem like she had invited him to her party as a little brother or something.

Mindy reached over and patted his thigh. "Yep, nothing can go on between us. That would be unprofessional." She let her hand linger there. Doug thought he would drive off the road. All the blood in his body shot to his penis and Mindy would have had to notice his state if she glanced down. Then he thought maybe she did because she said, "Oh," and quickly took her hand away, curling it with her other hand in the black void of her lap.

"So you never told me why you're wearing that... cloak."

"This? It's a ceremonial robe. I thought I told you about all this."

"Huh uh."

"This is my initiation week... at the Tabernacle. That's what the party's for. I invited you, don't you remember?"

"Of course, I thought you said it was just a get together. I didn't know it was something church related."

"You still want to come, don't you?"

"Definitely! I wouldn't miss it."

"It's for myself and two other girls. Want to drive to the Tabernacle? You said you've never seen it, right?"

"Sure. No, I haven't seen it."

"I'll write the directions down for you too. Or I could just come and pick you up."

"Yeah. That'd be great."

"Still want to see it?"

"Yeah."

She guided him through town and onto the state route and they veered off onto a couple of back roads, went past the Church of the New Covenant, and then turned onto a gravel road. The sign said, appropriately, "Tabernacle Dr." and, below that, "No Outlet." Somebody had taken it upon themselves to spray paint, in red, "666" over the "No Outlet" sign. Doug had seen things like that before and figured it wasn't anything new. He imagined all small towns were the same. There was always some place rumored to be the site of Satanic rituals and cults. He assumed it was more predominant the more religious the town was. Like yin and yang or whatever. For every Doug, there was somebody like Crank. But maybe even Crank was coming around.

Doug had to power the small car up a fairly steep hill.

"It's right up here," Mindy said.

He pulled the car to a stop when he ran out of gravel. He didn't see any type of church or building or anything.

"We'll have to do some walking. Just a little bit."

He turned the car off and they got out, the engine ticking down. He proffered the keys to Mindy but she said she didn't have anywhere to put them so he slid them into his pocket and felt very grown up. The woods were thick here and alive with the sounds of insects. Doug thought back to that strange thing he'd seen the other day and had a brief moment of panic. In the interim, he had managed to convince himself it was a deer but, thinking back on it, there was no way. Possibly a bear. Or some monstrous goat with a disease that rendered it vicious. Mindy didn't seem too worried. She took off her helmet and tossed it into the car. She ran her hands through her shiny hair. The voluminous black garb only accentuated how attractive her face was. It was as close to perfection as Doug had seen. Her hair was now a little bit ratty, she didn't look like she wore any make-up, and Doug thought he liked her better like this.

"Follow me," she said.

She led him down a narrow dirt trail for about a quarter of a mile.

"Why's this out in the middle of nowhere?"

"I don't know. Probably cheap rent."

"Why don't they just let you guys do your thing in the Church?"

"Don says this is better for focus. There are guys in the Church and all that. He seems to think we'd take some of the attention. Or vice versa, I guess."

"There aren't that many guys in the Church."

"No?"

"No. I mean, there are some children who go to Sunday school but the only one our age or... my age anyway, was a guy named Jim Lankmeyer and he's dead now. I guess there are some deacons and stuff but they're all older."

"Hm. Well then, maybe it was just to keep us away from you."

Doug almost laughed.

They reached the Tabernacle. It looked like it had been converted from a one room schoolhouse.

"It used to be a one room schoolhouse," Mindy said.

The building was pretty ramshackle looking.

"It's pretty rundown," Mindy said.

There weren't even any windows in it.

"Don says it's to help us keep focus. He's really about focus and discipline. No windows. Nothing to distract us. We just have to clean up a little bit every now and then."

"Are we going to go inside?" He was really curious about what the inside of this place looked like. He thought he might explode if he went in, knowing it was mostly just a few girls here all the time.

"I don't have any keys. I just wanted you to see the outside of it."

"Pretty neat."

"I guess."

Doug sneaked a peak at Mindy. She had beads of sweat standing up on her forehead.

"Aren't you hot in that thing?"

"It is pretty warm. I guess I could take it off. I don't have to wear it all the time or anything. It's not like I'm a nun or something. But we had a lesson here earlier and I didn't have time to go home and change." She wiped some sweat from her upper lip with the back of her hand. "It *is* hot, though."

She unfastened a drawstring around the neck, allowing the robe to fall open. Then she pulled it up over her head. Doug was expecting clothes. What she wore instead were a pair of white hip hugger underwear and a white sports bra.

She noticed him gaping and shrugged. He must not have done very well at hiding his surprise or lust. "Come on, this is less than what you'd see if you went to the beach. Why's it okay to wear a swimsuit outside but not your underwear?"

"You've got a point." Doug's penis again stiffened in his pants.

"You have been to the beach, haven't you?"

Doug hadn't. He didn't say anything. Apparently he didn't need to.

"Oh my God, you *haven't*, have you? And you've never seen a girl in her underwear?"

Doug stared somewhere past her, not wanting to make eye contact.

"Come on. You can be honest with me. Besides, if you haven't seen a girl in her underwear before then you have now. Right?"

She had a point. "Yeah," he said, looking at her tight stomach. "I guess I have seen a girl in her underwear."

"I'm sorry. Is this making you nervous? I didn't mean anything by it. You said it yourself—it's hot out."

And it was. He could see the light sheen of sweat gathered on the rounded tops of her breasts.

"Ready to go back?"

He nodded. She didn't seem to mind that he kept looking at her. She led the way through the woods and Doug stared at her firm ass the entire time. He couldn't take his eyes off it. Occasionally she would glance back and smile like she knew what he was doing. They got back to the car way too soon. He expected her to put her robe back on and get back into the car but she didn't. She tossed the robe into the car and went around to the trunk.

"Keys?" she said.

Doug reached into his pocket and grabbed the keys.

"You've about got this driving thing down, huh?"

"I think I got the hang of it."

"So we'll do the highway on Wednesday and then I think we can manage to count your time when you come to my initiation ceremony on Friday and that should be about it. Unless you wanted to spend the next hour or so driving around. Do you think you need that?"

"If you have things to do, that's fine. Like I said, I think I've got it."

"I don't really have anything to do. It's just that... driving around Clover gets kind of boring, you know."

She slid the key into the trunk and popped the lid.

"Want a beer?" she said.

Doug wouldn't mind having a beer at all.

Before he could even answer, Mindy had reached into a cooler and handed him a can of Miller Lite.

"Thanks," he said. He popped the top and took a long sip. She did the same. She put the frosty can on her stomach. He watched her nipples tighten against the fabric of her bra.

"So this girl you're seeing tonight, is it pretty serious?"

"Serious?"

"Yeah. I mean, she's your girlfriend, right?"

"Oh," Doug laughed. "It's a girl and she's my friend but we're not going out or anything."

"Have you asked her?"

"Um, no, I've never thought about it."

"You don't like her in that way?"

"I don't think so."

"You don't *think* so?"

Doug started to get nervous. He took another drink of beer, hoping that would help.

"Is she pretty?"

"She's pretty in a certain way."

"What's 'in a certain way' mean?"

"Um, not like you."

Now Mindy laughed. "Not like me?"

"She's pretty in an attainable way."

"Attainable?"

"Yeah. Like if I asked her out she might actually say yes."

"Ah." Mindy looked away and downed most of her beer. Doug was sort of hoping she would say something to refute him, at least to give him hope. "That's not a good way to think of girls, Doug."

"Like what."

"Like 'attainable'. How do you think that would make her feel?"

"I guess it's moot anyway."

"Why's that?"

"I mean I might as well just get used to having girls as friends until it's time to get married. Everything I could do with a girl except for talk seems like it's a sin."

"Sex before marriage is a sin. But that leaves a lot out."

"Lust is also a sin."

"But I like to think of it as a lesser sin."

Mindy took the keys to the front seat of the car and stuck them in the ignition. The beer had made Doug somewhat bolder and he watched her rounded ass bent over the seat, the muscles in her legs drawn tight. She turned the radio on. It was something loud with a steady bass beat. Different than whatever kind of metal music she was listening to before. Doug thought this sounded like something people would listen to at a rave.

"How is lust a lesser sin?" he asked.

"Well, you have to make a distinction between thinking and doing. I mean, murder is a sin, definitely. But who hasn't thought about killing someone from time to time? Granted, if you think about it all the time it might mean you're screwed but, otherwise, I think it's normal and certainly not anything you would end up burning in hell for. So, really, what's lust except for thinking about sex? You're a teenage boy. I *know* you've thought about sex. In fact, I think you have to. To know why you don't want to commit that sin and to realize yet another beautiful aspect to marriage, you *have* to think about sex. About what it can create and the harm it can do. It's like that game the Church likes its members to play—*Redemption*. That forces people to think about sex. And it also forces them to refuse it. To not give into the sin. You've played it, haven't you?"

"A little."

"And you can't admit to me that you didn't have a hard-on

sometimes."

Mindy using that word caught him by surprise. He almost choked on his beer. "A what?"

"A hard-on, Doug. An erection?"

"Oh."

"So?"

"So what?"

"So did you ever get hard while you were playing that?"

Now he felt the redness creep back up into his cheeks. "Yeah," he said. "I guess... sometimes."

Mindy moved closer to him. "Want another beer?"

"Why not?"

She reached into the trunk and pulled out two more beers. "You know, mostly, it's people from the Church who are posing as the prostitutes in that game, so they can monitor you." She moved close to him again. "It might have even been me."

Doug swallowed hard.

"Do you think dancing's a sin?"

"Not always."

She began to move slowly to the beat of the music from the car. She pressed her damp back to him, bringing her butt against the front of his pants. He put his hands on her hips to try and force her away, not wanting her to feel his hardness, and she grabbed his hands and clamped them down on her hips so each one was half on her underwear and half on the stickiness of her skin. She moved her ass against the front of his pants. He moved his hands farther to the front of her hips, feeling bone beneath the skin, and pulled her against him. She pressed harder until his clothed penis was between her ass cheeks. She looked over her shoulder, throwing her hair out of her face, and said, "We're just dancing, Doug. Just dancing."

He was beyond speech. He wondered if this was an invitation to do anything. He wondered if he *would* do anything. No. He had to draw the line somewhere. But, Jesus, there were so many things he wanted to do with this girl. Already, he had done more than he ever had before.

She continued to move her ass faster and harder against him. He felt ready to split out of his pants and through her thin underwear. He moved his head into her neck to smell her sweat and perfume scent. He moved his hands up to her breasts, expecting her to push them down. She didn't and he could feel her nipples against his palms, the weight and softness of her breasts like nothing he'd ever felt before. Now he was sitting on the tailgate of the car and she was on his lap, her head practically on his shoulder, her legs spread out to either side. He moved his hand between her legs and momentarily felt her damp warmth before she pulled his hand up to her thigh. She continued to move against him and when he looked down he saw that her underwear's waistband had come down a bit and he could see the crack of her ass. He knew he was going to do something at that point and thought that he really should make her stop but just when he thought about forcing her she said, again, "Just dancing, Doug. Just dancing..." And his penis stiffened as much as it could and then released, warm and slimy in his tight underwear. She danced on him for a few more seconds and then slowly got off, pulling her panties from the crack in her butt and pulling the waistband up.

"Now," she said, "I bet we both feel better and no sins were committed. Right?"

Doug wasn't sure about that but said, "Right," anyway.

"I guess we should probably go, huh?"

"You're the instructor," Doug said.

"So did you want to drive to your friend's house or home?" Mindy smiled at him.

"Um, I need to go home and grab some things. She lives right next door so don't worry about it."

Doug got behind the wheel. Mindy put her robe and helmet on and they drove off.

Twenty-seven

Doug's mother sat in the living room, the TV blaring. That horrible show, *Johnny Got His Gun*, was on. Doug didn't get the appeal of it. He didn't say hi. Neither did she. He went up to his room and sat on his bed. He took deep breaths. He didn't know what had happened with Mindy. He was pretty sure he was supposed to feel bad but he felt good. Really good. Except for the sticky mess in his underwear. He thought about calling Crank to tell him what had happened. But Crank would probably just laugh at him.

His breathing still didn't feel right. He felt out of control. There was a moment with Mindy when he would have done anything she asked him to. There was a moment when he had to fight the urge to do whatever he wanted to with her. He knew he would never do that, but the thought was there. Of course it was. That was why it was a sin to indulge in sex and sexual thoughts. Because you only wanted more. After a while, it probably didn't even matter what you did or who you did it with.

He had to change pants and underwear before he went to Whitney's.

Whitney.

Jesus. He thought he was attracted to her too. Even though she was the complete opposite of Mindy.

He disrobed from the waist down. His pubic hair was still a damp mess. He dried himself off with his underwear as best as possible then buried the soiled clothes in the bottom of his closet. He'd have to wash them himself when his mom left the house for something longer than a cigarette run.

He put fresh pants and underwear on, slipped his shoes back on. He looked at his computer. He had absolutely no desire to play *Redemption.* What was the point now, anyway? If he couldn't fend off temptation in real life, then there was absolutely no hope of him doing it in the game, where the risks weren't even real.

He went back downstairs.

"Where are you going?" his mother asked.

"Maybe over to Crank's."

"You're walking?"

"Yeah. I can't *drive* by myself."

"Why'd you change pants?"

"The other ones were dirty."

"You just put them on this morning. You have to change pants for Crank?"

"I just like these better, okay?"

"They're exactly like the other ones. Same brand. Same style. Same color."

"Why does it matter?"

"Because I want to know what you've been doing."

"I just came back from driving lessons. You can call and ask."

"I don't want to bother them. They're busy doing both the Lord's work and teaching people to drive."

"Then you believe me?"

"I still want to know why you changed pants."

"Maybe it's embarrassing, okay?"

"See. That's all you had to say."

"I might not be back until later." His hand on the front doorknob, he was nearly free.

"And Doug?"

He gritted his teeth. Turned to face his mother.

"Be careful. People are dying left and right."

He was glad the obligatory warning about the evils of the world was the only thing she had to say. He forced a smile and said, "I think I'll be okay."

"You'd better be. I don't know what I'd do if anything ever happened to you."

Doug stepped outside and closed the door behind him.

Twenty-eight

Amanda awoke at dusk. The sweet smell of honeysuckle floated in through the window. She distinctly remembered drawing the curtains and the blinds but had probably left the windows open with hopes of Lawrence Kansas coming back. Of course, she didn't really think it was Lawrence Kansas. It was that other person. She didn't know exactly who that person was and wasn't sure it really mattered. He made her feel good. Just thinking about what they had done the past two nights made her wet. She thought about touching herself but was afraid that would dull her sensitivity and then it wouldn't be as powerful the next time they did something.

She wished she knew his name. Wished she knew who to thank. It was only a few days ago she had felt so trapped. And now she felt so free. Like she could do anything. *Feel* anything. Right now she felt blissful. Just the thought of being with that mysterious creature again made her smile.

She felt anxious. Surely he would come back for her. He had told her she was to be a witness. And while she had witnessed one of their rituals, she didn't think that was the only thing she was supposed to witness. She hadn't thought the Church would be mixed up in all the things happening to her, but it was. Even though it was a haze, she could still remember much of what had happened to her at the Church before the funeral ceremonies. She would have thought that seemed evil. But now she saw it for the beautiful thing it was.

Beautiful things were all around her. They probably always had been, but she couldn't see them beyond Perry and her diseased mother. Now the veil, along with most of her other clothing, had been lifted.

Yes. Beautiful things were everywhere.

Maybe she just needed to seek them out.

She slid out of her clothes and left them in a heap on the floor of her living room. She opened the front door and walked out into the fragrant night.

Twenty-nine

Crank powered his bike through Doug's suburb, a case of Old Milwaukee strapped to the back of the seat, hidden by flapping plastic bags, all of it from America Pantry. He couldn't figure out why anyone would want to live in these horrible suburbs. Even in a small town like Clover, it still felt like there were too many people too close together, watching you.

He saw a naked woman wandering down the sidewalk and stopped the bike a few feet in front of her. Initially he was just going to ogle her, maybe ask if he wanted him to fuck her, but as she got closer he saw that her body was covered in scratches and bruises.

"Hey, lady! You okay?" he called.

She quickly turned her head toward him as though she hadn't even noticed he was there until he said something, and then came padding over. She didn't look at all like she was in trouble. She looked ecstatic.

"Are you okay?" he asked again.

She now stood within arm's length of him. "Oh yes. Why wouldn't I be? I feel ... I feel *great*."

Crank couldn't help but stare at her breasts, her hips, her well-trimmed pubic mound. As if hypnotized, he reached out to touch her breast. She wasn't as young as he preferred, but she was still put together pretty nicely and probably only on the near side of thirty, if that. She gently touched his hand and placed it on the grip of his bike.

"I'm sorry," she said, "but my body is not for you. It is for the powerful one. The one who... changes."

"Whatever. You're fucked up, lady."

Crank revved the bike with a twist of the grip and roared off in the direction of Doug's house. By the time he reached Doug's street, he was shaken. *It is for the powerful one. The one who changes.* Like that guy at Chloe's the one night? What had she said his name was? Daniel? Did she even say? Did it matter? Crazy shit was finally happening in Clover. That was what mattered to Crank.

Thirty

Doug raised his hand to knock on Whitney's front door when he heard her say, "I'm around here."

"Oh. Hi."

"Hi. Follow me."

Doug still felt out of it. Until his encounter with Mindy earlier, he'd been looking forward to seeing Whitney, even though he had no idea what pretense it was under. She had certainly been nice to him the other morning but that didn't really mean she liked him. He thought she was cute but, regardless of what he had done with Mindy, sex before marriage was still out of the question. He supposed they could just be friends and talk, but that was only if she turned out to be less crazy than he thought she was.

He followed her through the back yard. Their street was at the edge of the neighborhood and there wasn't anything but woods behind it. He smelled fire. She continued leading him toward the smell. Once they entered the woods he saw the fire burning. A quilt was thrown on the ground a decent distance from the fire.

She reached the quilt and stopped. Doug could smell something that went beyond the perfume of nature. Incense, maybe. She turned around to face Doug. He said hi again.

"You don't have to keep saying that."

"Okay. How are you?"

She rolled her eyes and said, "Fine, Doug. I'm... fine. How are you?"

"Confused."

"I know you're probably wondering why I wanted you to come over. Especially when I've been such a bitch to you at the store."

"Yeah, kinda. But that was nice what you did for me yesterday. I think you kept me out of a lot of trouble. Mom didn't say anything."

"Okay, yeah, you're welcome." She breathed shakily. "I want you to fuck me."

Doug's face turned red. He immediately felt really excited and really scared. He said, "Ummm."

"Look, I know you may not find me attractive but you're a boy so it shouldn't really matter. You told me you've never done it and neither have I so I think it's something we need to do together."

"I can't." But already his mind was racing. He didn't know if he was saying that because of what he did with Mindy—like maybe he really, physically *couldn't*—or if he said it because of how he felt about sex before marriage. Or because of how the *Church* felt about sex before marriage.

"Why not?" She didn't look hurt. She looked... maybe angry?

"It's a sin."

"That is shit." She advanced on him, grabbed him around the neck and planted her lips on his. Then her tongue was in his mouth and she was grinding her bony hips against him. It felt really good but nothing was happening and he knew if they were to proceed it would only end in embarrassment. But he liked what they were doing and they sunk down onto the blanket. The fire crackled beside them and the insects made music in the woods around them and the incense continued to breathe its perfumed breath. Time melted away. Whitney was very good with her hands. Probably since Doug didn't respond the way she wanted him to, she undid his pants and pulled them down, kissing him on his penis. He should have told her to stop. Why didn't he? Because it felt so good. And he would become erect briefly before it would deflate. He had no doubt he would have done what Whitney wanted him to if he had been able.

He heard a buzzing in the distance and thought it sounded like Crank's dirt bike but he dismissed it, trying to supplant it with the sounds of Whitney's slurping.

Then he heard, "Whoa! Fuck that throat, bro!" and any hope he had of an erection was gone completely.

Thirty-one

Whitney quickly stood up, wiping her mouth and turning her back to them. Crank continued his crooked walk toward the fire. Doug was already standing, tucked, and buttoned. He felt bad. He was pretty sure Whitney was embarrassed.

"Girl's got skills!" Crank said. Whatever he was on, it was making him shout.

Doug punched him on the arm.

"What? You're all over the place. First that bitch at the driving school and now sweet little Whitney. Soon I'm not going to have anything on you."

Whitney, realizing they probably just weren't going to leave, turned back around and joined them.

"Great timing," she said.

"I didn't realize tonight was the night you were going to deflower our precious Dougie. You can keep going. I'll wait."

"No," Doug and Whitney said simultaneously.

"All right, when are we going to start drinking?"

Neither Whitney nor Doug answered him.

"Right," he said. "We need something to drink and I left the beer on the bike. Whitney? Would you be a good little woman and..."

He couldn't finish before she had spit on him, the bulk of it landing in his increasingly bizarre hair.

"Dammit." He turned and walked back toward the house.

"Did you... invite him?" Doug asked.

"Yes. Well, he kind of invited himself. He has ways of making you tell him things you don't want to."

"Like?"

"Like I just mentioned you might be coming over tonight and then it was like he was there. I was assuming he would bring somebody and we could sneak off and be alone. Actually, I was pretty sure we'd be finished by the time he got here. Besides, what was that about you and the driving instructor?"

She sounded mad. Doug certainly didn't want to give her any indication of what had happened earlier.

"Is that why you couldn't get it up?" she practically spat. "Because you were fucking her? Was I licking some other girl's cunt off your dick?"

"Calm down. She's just a woman who invited me to a get together."

"A woman. Is she like fifty?"

"I don't know. She's in her twenties, I guess."

"But she's cute, right? What's her name?"

He was glad she asked two questions so he didn't have to answer the first. "Mindy. Um, I don't remember her last name."

"And?"

"And what?"

"Is she cute?"

"She's all right. I don't think she's really interested in me."

"You're so full of shit. Mindy Astan's the only Mindy I know and she's gorgeous."

Doug didn't say anything.

"So Mindy Astan invites you to a party and you don't think she's interested?"

"It's not really a party party. She's a church person like me. It's a graduation party or something. She'll probably have family there and everything. It's really no big deal."

"So are you allowed to bring a date?"

"No, um, she told me to come by myself."

"Then it's a date!"

"How did you turn this around?" Crank was shuffling through the yard. "You invited Crank. Crank's like... the Devil or something. And if I hadn't come, which wasn't a definite, you'd be alone with him."

She rolled her eyes. "And probably getting fucked."

"It feels too heavy around here," Crank said. "I've got the prescription for *that*."

He sat the case of beer on the ground, savagely ripped it open, and pulled one out. He also pulled out a pack of cigarettes and lit one up.

"Can I bum one?" Whitney asked.

He offered the pack to her. She took one and he offered the pack to Doug. Doug shook his head.

They sat on stumps were arranged around the fire and were silent while they sipped their beers.

Thirty-two

Amanda continued to walk as if hypnotized. She realized why she thought the air smelled so fragrant. It was blood. It was all around her. Maybe on her. Maybe she even smelled the blood coursing inside her. It smelled delicious. When she reached the edge of town, a car, a red convertible with the top down, pulled up beside her.

Mindy and Kristen sat in the front seat. Angie sat in back.

"Amanda!" Kristen called.

Amanda was already walking over to them.

"Hop in."

Amanda hopped in the back without opening the door.

Mindy hit the accelerator and they were speeding outside Clover.

"Here, take this." Angie proffered a pill to Amanda.

"What is it?"

"It doesn't matter. It'll make you feel great."

"I already feel great." And she did. The night was warm, the air rushed over her naked skin. The only way she could feel better was if Lawrence Kansas were here.

"This'll make you feel even better."

There certainly wasn't any harm in that. She took the pill and, after only a few miles, it was like a whole other level opened up inside her and she did feel even better. She felt powerful. Indestructible.

"This is our last night of freedom," Angie said. "Tomorrow we must begin preparations."

"Preparations for what?"

"To become brides of Satan. To pledge ourselves only to him."

"Glorious," Amanda said. Laughed and then said, "Glory glory."

"So you must witness this as well."

"Of course," Amanda said, knowing that to witness would also mean to take part in whatever they had planned.

Eventually everything began to feel unreal.

They drove to a strip club in Newport. Mindy and Kristen got out of the car and approached a group of frat boys on their way into the club. Amanda thought they looked common and normal. They seemed reluctant at first. Then Amanda corrected herself. They looked common and normal, but they also looked like meat. Young, healthy meat. And she thought about the youthful, rock hard cocks undoubtedly hidden in their clean boxer shorts. Once Mindy brought them back to their car and they caught a glimpse of Amanda, naked and semi-conscious, they were ready to follow them anywhere.

The frat boys piled into their huge SUV. There had to be at least eight of them, all smiling and laughing.

On the way back into Clover, Amanda lay in the backseat while Angie buried her head between Amanda's legs and lapped at her vagina. The sensation lasted, building until they reached that place in the woods, never climaxing.

The frat boys, drunk and giggling, followed them into the Tabernacle.

Soon no one was wearing any clothes. Things were blurred and swirling around Amanda. Everyone was sweating and moaning. Cocks slid easily into her mouth and her dripping cunt and even into her asshole. The same thing happened to the girls with her, their eyes ferocious and intense, riding every moment, every thrust, every moan. It reached a fevered pitch. One cock filled Amanda's ass pushing her just to the brink of pain, while another cock stared her in the face, semen shooting out of it, onto her nose, her lips, dribbling warmly onto her breasts.

Then there were screams.

Explosions of blood. Red mist hanging in the candlelight. The blood coated the walls, mixing with the semen on the floor, on the girls, in the girls.

She didn't know when the goats had arrived. But they were there too. White fur quickly pinked, before they too became part of the sacrifice and just when Amanda thought she couldn't take it anymore, the beast was there, lapping at each of them, filling them with pleasures the frat boys never could.

The night went on.

Thirty-three

Doug made it through the first half of his beer fairly quickly. The only sounds were the crackling fire and the insects. He wasn't sure he'd ever not heard Crank be quiet this long.

"So," Doug said, lifting the beer in front of his eyes, "you probably could've stolen it from the cooler. Then it'd be cold."

"Beer's beer, man. Patel was there. I had to take it from the store room. Sometimes it's a good thing he makes me keep my bike back there. I really want to fuck his wife. Mainly because I've never fucked anything except white girls but she's pretty cute."

"Is that racism or reverse racism?" Whitney said.

"Fuck if I know. It's love."

"That I'm sure it's not."

"You're a bitch, Whitney."

"Thanks. You're an asshole."

"I know."

"What am I?" Doug asked, feeling left out.

Crank said "prude" and Whitney said "creepy" at the same time. Doug drank the rest of the beer and tossed the can into the fire.

"I think I will have one of those cigarettes."

Crank tossed the pack to him. They each took one. Doug didn't really have any idea how to smoke it but he played it as cool as he could and managed not to cough.

"There. Is that less... prudish?"

"Sure, man, I guess. I didn't mean anything by it. You've just always been that way. I blame your mom... and Jesus."

"It's all been a personal decision."

"Whatever. If you hadn't had your mom there shoving it down your throat every day, you wouldn't be any more religious than me."

"But aren't you the one who expressed interest in coming to church with me?" Saying this in front of Whitney would probably embarrass him. Doug waited for him to make some kind of stupid excuse but he didn't.

"Well, yeah, I never believed in any of that shit before but I saw something that really scared me." He described his encounter with Chloe and Daniel in overly lurid detail, as crudely as possible. Doug felt like even Whitney was probably blushing. When he finished he said, "So that's it. I figure if there are evil supernatural kinds of things that can happen, then there must be something good, too."

Whitney said, "So you think you saw the Devil and now you want to go to church?"

"That's about right."

"And you think that's going to help you how?"

"It's going to make me righteous."

Doug laughed, opened another beer. "I think maybe you need to go into rehab."

"That's not a very nice thing to say." Whitney took another cigarette and lit it.

"You're taking *his* side?"

"I'm not taking anybody's side. But I think he's right. I think he saw the Devil."

But Doug thought she *was* taking Crank's side. He didn't know what was going on. Anger flashed up through his cheeks. Something had happened. He didn't know what. Maybe Whitney had gone into the station today and found Crank there and they'd spent an hour or so talking. Talking about him. Planning this prank or whatever it was. He stood up.

"Okay, yep, it's really funny that I go to church. It's really funny that I've tried to live a clean life and all that. It's all hilarious that I believe anything because you both obviously believe nothing. Well, I'm leaving. When you grow up and decide to treat me like a friend then you should give me a call or something."

He walked away.

"Doug, don't go!" Whitney called. He kept walking. "I still need to talk to you." But that was probably all just part of the joke. Something they'd spent a lot of time planning and now that he wasn't buying into it, they would do anything to see it through, even though neither one of them did anything but waste time anyway.

Thirty-four

Doug went deeper into the woods, Crank's and Whitney's calls for him like pitiful music. He couldn't go back home yet. His mom would still be awake and having just drank a beer and smoked a cigarette, he knew she would smell it on him. Maybe not the cigarette smoke, but definitely the beer. She had a remarkable sense of smell for a smoker. Maybe he should just go back to Crank and Whitney. He knew he'd overreacted. He didn't know what was wrong with him.

Only that wasn't exactly true. He was growing up. That was the problem. And he was tired of everyone still treating him like a kid. There were plenty of adults in the Church, so he didn't know why he should feel his belief was somehow childish, like God was someone like Santa Claus or the Easter Bunny. And he definitely didn't think it was any reason for Whitney and Crank to gang up on him. But that was what had happened. The beauty of democracy, he thought. If two out of three people think a certain way, then that must be truth, law.

It wasn't like he had a lot of other options. Crank had been his friend forever. And even though he'd only recently re-met Whitney, he thought there could be something there. Not necessarily a boyfriend-girlfriend something, but she seemed as weird and withdrawn as he felt most of the time and he was always under the assumption those people seemed to be more interesting than the loud and obnoxious types of people—at least for anything other than being a spectacle.

Their plaintive cries grew farther away. Doug wiped a cobweb from his face and stopped, listening.

Now he couldn't hear anything. That made him feel even worse.

How quickly they forget, he thought.

He wasn't just angry at Crank and Whitney. He was angrier with himself. The way he'd been acting over the past few days made him feel like he was mocking his religion even more than they were. Maybe it had started with the drinking. It had clouded his judgment. The drinking and the turning eighteen and the driving lessons and Mindy. Mindy. Mindy. Mindy. He still wasn't sure he wouldn't do anything she asked him to do. It was more than just being beautiful. She was older. She was part of the Church, practically a nun. In short, she was almost as close to being a role model as Pastor Don. Maybe even more so because she was closer to his age.

Maybe Crank was the reason he had done the things he had done. Maybe he just needed to avoid Crank. They were, in a way, the closest of friends, but they didn't really have anything in common anymore except for memories. Doug was adult enough to know that memories couldn't sustain a friendship. It was like a married couple who couldn't talk about anything except for their kids. Doomed.

Why did everything have to be so difficult? Maybe things would change when he went to college in the fall. This was Kentucky, after all, so he was sure there would be some kind of campus organization for students of faith. He would need it. From what he had heard, the temptations of college life would surely test that faith in ways it had never been tested before.

He continued walking. He figured he would go down to the

creek and find a big rock to sit down on and watch the moon and collect his thoughts.

Sort some things out.

He heard twigs snap behind him and... was that panting?

He felt a moment of panic. What if it was a wild dog? He didn't have anything to fight it off with. He wasn't sure he could outrun a dog. He knew it was dumb to turn around but he would have felt even dumber if he just took off running through the woods and it turned out he wasn't running from anything other than his imagination.

He turned around.

It wasn't a dog.

It was so much larger. And terrifying.

He thought he'd found what he'd nearly run into the other day.

Thirty-five

After walking into the woods far enough to lose sight of the fire, Crank said, "Just let him go."

"Let him go?" Whitney said. "After what we were getting ready to talk about you want us to just let him go? Why? So we can read about him in the paper after his mutilated body is found?"

"He's not going to stop. He's pissed. You don't know Doug like I do. He'd say he never gets mad and if you didn't know him very well, you'd probably think that. But here's what happens: He does get mad. It doesn't take much to set him off, you just have to know what that is. One thing is that church shit. The other thing is his mother. He doesn't yell or anything but he's real stubborn. If I don't call him and tell him how sorry and shit I am, he would *never* call me. And I don't mean it would just take him a while. I mean that I would be completely dead to him. See, we're both dead to him right now. He's already making plans for the future that don't involve us. I guarantee it. I know him. Better than anyone."

"Okay then." She threw her hands up into the air. "We'll just... let him go and hope nothing happens to him."

"He's probably already home by now anyway. It's not like he has any place else to go."

"Maybe we should go there, then."

"Anything we could say to him is only going to make it worse."

"That still doesn't solve my problem, does it?"

"Are you really serious about this shit?"

"Aren't you? I thought that was the whole reason we were going to talk to him."

"I know I saw something crazy at Chloe's and I know it wasn't drug-inspired but I still don't know if I buy into your whole crazy conspiracy theory."

"It's not a theory."

"It's still way out there."

"Is it? You want to go in and ask my mom? You know that's why she doesn't leave the house, don't you? Because she would talk. Everyone else in this town, everyone who goes to the Church anyway, knows the truth, and if you asked any of them what that truth was, they'd talk around it. That's how I got out of Brentwood House. I told Mom I'd go along with it. I went there in the first place because I refused to go along with it. When I asked her to come and get me out, the only thing she asked was, 'Are you still a virgin?'"

"And you are?"

"Yes. And that makes things dangerous for me. I don't know what I can do to make you believe me. Something big is going to happen and it's going to be horrible and the two people who are currently in the most danger are me and Doug. And he knows absolutely nothing about what's going on."

"Well, I can help you with your problem."

"Jesus." Whitney put a hand on her forehead, almost surprised it had taken Crank this long to come on to her. Definitely surprised at what her answer was going to be.

"I didn't think Jesus was your problem."

"I'm going to need *a lot* more beer."

"It's waiting. Besides, maybe Doug will change his mind and come back before we do anything. Maybe you can con him into it."

"A girl shouldn't have to do that, though, should she? *Con* a guy into fucking her?"

Crank shrugged. "Some guys are weird."

They went back to the slightly dwindled fire. As Whitney drank, she thought of the photos and drawings her mother had shown her on the day she freaked out. The day they took her away.

"You are his daughter," she had said. "And you will enroll in the Tabernacle so you may offer yourself to him like a good daughter should. And if you're the best, which you will be, then he will choose you as his bride. But if he smells any taint on you..." It took Whitney a while to pull the red photo into focus, to make out the flayed skin, the bones peeking through, the organs glistening within.

Before they were finished with their first beer, she had moved close to Crank, leaned into him, whispered into his ear. Anything would be better than offering herself to that man, that beast, that thing that called itself the Devil.

Thirty-six

Doug wanted to bolt as soon as he saw the thing but there was something keeping him rooted to the ground. Part of it was fear, sure. But another part of it was that he was looking at something he had never seen before. It kind of looked like a werewolf only it had large horns.

I'm looking at the Devil, he thought.

And he thought this thing appearing at this exact moment was the first true sign he'd ever had that Good and Evil, God and Satan actually existed.

But that wasn't enough to keep him there. And while he had a moment where he didn't think he would be able to move, the way it always happened in dreams, that wasn't the case and he watched the thing take a great sniff in the air and as soon as Doug took off, he heard the thing behind him, covering twice as much ground as he was.

Now he really wished he hadn't drunk that one beer as fast as he did and it was probably the cigarette making his heart jump around in his chest and his lungs burn. Worse than watching out for the trees was trying not to trip over everything on the ground. He ran in a diagonal pattern, toward what he thought was his house. If he were closer to the Church, he would have tried to go there. But he thought his house might be the safest reachable thing. Once he was inside, his mom wouldn't care that maybe he smelled like beer because he would have such great news for her. And they could rejoice that he was safe and their beliefs were justified and they were both now aware of the awesome fight that lay before them.

Just that momentary thought, that second's lack of concentration on his surroundings, was enough to trip him up and send him sprawling.

The beast was on him as soon as he hit the ground.

Doug smelled something rotting and something wild. The beast was damp and humid. Doug closed his eyes against the pain he knew was inevitable but then he thought that if this thing, the Devil, was going to kill him, kill him and eat his soul, then he should look it in the eye. If he made eye contact with it, then the Devil could look inside him and see that his soul was pure and that, even if it killed him, there was nothing else it would get from him.

Doug opened his eyes and was not surprised to see the thing staring deeply into his eyes. Whatever this thing was, it was more man than beast. He had his massive mouth open, ready to clamp down on Doug's throat, but then he paused. He began sniffing Doug, keeping him held down with his massive hands. He sniffed down Doug's chest. Sniffed down to his crotch and spent a lot of time there, making it even more uncomfortable for Doug.

Then an amazing thing happened.

The man, Doug was now convinced he was the Devil, stood up, growled, and went loping off into the forest.

The moon was fat overhead. Doug's heart hammered in his chest. A smile spread itself across his face. Jesus had saved him. He was sure of it.

But what about Crank? Had Jesus saved him too?

Of course he had. Jesus saves everyone he can. Maybe Crank hadn't been lying. Maybe he and Whitney hadn't been trying to play some horrible joke on Doug. Really, that wouldn't be like Crank at all. He was dumb and insensitive but he was probably about the least mean-spirited person Doug knew. He didn't treat girls in a way that was exactly nice but that was probably more his hormones than any kind of mean intent.

Maybe he'd overreacted.

Or maybe he just felt jubilant and relieved he had escaped.

Well, he hadn't exactly escaped yet. He wasn't sure the Devil wouldn't come back for him but, in a way, he was. He felt protected. He probably still shouldn't go back home. His mom was probably already suspicious of him. He didn't want her lording over him for the rest of the summer. Besides, he wanted to share this experience with someone and thought it would be more meaningful if he shared it with Crank and Whitney.

He took a deep breath and stood up.

He didn't want to go back the way he had come so he continued in a circular pattern, winding up a few houses down from his own and then cutting along the edge of the woods, just far enough under cover so no one in their back yard or looking out their windows would notice him and grow suspicious. Blood continued to pound in his ears and when he reached the area behind his own house, he paused and looked at it. He'd never really seen it from this angle and he had one of those moments where looking at something that should have been really familiar seemed really foreign. From here he could see the fire crackling behind Chloe's house. It had grown so small, he wondered if they were still there. He knew they had come after him but figured both of them would have gotten tired of looking for him fairly quickly. Maybe Crank had just left after that.

Or maybe something terrible had happened to them.

Maybe the Devil had come back that way.

Maybe he had killed both of them.

Only the Devil didn't just kill. He sacrificed. The blood and skin of humans was used as something like currency. Something to make him even stronger.

He shook his head. Where did that train of thought come from?

He walked toward the fire. Mostly smoke now, he could smell it almost as much as see it. The moon overhead afforded more light than the fire.

He heard Whitney making a sound and had a horrible vision of the Devil mawing her. He sped his pace, standing nearly on top of the fire after a couple of seconds.

Not the Devil.

Crank.

Whitney was on her back on the ground. Crank pumped away between her legs, his pale buttocks practically glowing in the night. Doug thought about shouting, stopping them. But what did it matter? Isn't this what he knew would happen? He felt stupid for ever doubting his thoughts about them. He turned and walked back to his house. By this time his mom would probably be asleep in front of the TV anyway. He'd probably be able to sneak past her and go up to his room. He didn't think about playing *Redemption.* The excitement he'd felt only moments before had dissipated entirely. Replaced with... what?

Nothing.

He knew his faith had waned over the past week. Maybe it had been happening longer than that.

He'd renew it. He'd throw himself into the Church even moreso. He'd begin school in the fall. If there wasn't already a campus program, he'd start one. He'd meet other people like himself. People who didn't lie to their best friends. People who wanted to do something besides drink and rut. People who were not Crank.

Thirty-seven

Whitney didn't think it would take as long as it did. Crank kept thrusting and thrusting. He would pull out, position her how he wanted, jerk himself off a little bit, and then enter her again. He tried to put it in her ass at one point and she hissed, "No." Most of her clothes were still on and they were soaked with sweat. There had been a fleeting moment of pleasure but that had given way to pain. She was pretty sure he was rubbing her raw. The pain blossomed and then became a less stinging dullness. After what felt like two hours, Crank pulled out, yanked the condom off, and grabbed her by the back of her head.

Did he want her to put him in her mouth? She shook her head. Kept her mouth closed. He began jerking himself off, the other hand keeping her head held in place. He quickly exploded onto her face. She had never even seen a porno before so this took her by surprise. She lurched away, almost went into the fire and wiped her sleeve across her face.

"Asshole!" she yelled.

"What? I just did you a favor." He looked pathetic standing there with his not extremely large cock drooping below his stomach, his pants around his ankles.

"Yeah, well, thanks for the fucking favor." She grabbed her underwear up off the ground and began walking toward her house, flipping Crank off.

"There's still stuff we need to talk about," he yelled. "What about Doug!"

"Fuck the both of you."

Crank pulled his pants up and watched her go into the darkened house.

Tuesday June 17

Thirty-eight

Doug opened the door. It was never locked. Hadn't been locked for as long as he could remember. The house was darkened but he could see the swirling colors from the television in the living room. He thought about trying to sneak past his mom but he didn't really care. So what if she smelled beer on his breath? That didn't mean he was ever going to drink again. He could convince her of that.

Glancing over at the couch, she wasn't there.

In her place was Deacon Pork.

That changed things a little. If he tried to argue with Deacon Pork, he would probably be put in a head lock or something. Besides fear, a lot of things went through his head. Was his mother okay? It wasn't like her to leave the house. Especially not after dark. Why was Pork here? Was it possible that Pork was seeing his mother? That was a repulsive thought and he couldn't recall if Pork had a wife or not. If he did, she didn't come to church. Doug couldn't imagine Pork standing for something like that.

"Where's Mom?" Doug asked.

Pork, who had been eyeing him ever since Doug had entered the room, now stood up from the couch, still wearing that skin tight wrestling singlet. Maybe church was the only place he didn't wear the singlet.

"Maybe she went out looking for you."

"Why?"

"Because it's after midnight and she worries about you."

"I'm eighteen. If she did, that's ridiculous. Why are you here, anyway?"

"Your mother had to do a few things. She wanted me to stay here and wait for you. Make sure you remembered all the things we talked about the other day. About wrestling the devil and the demons and the... the evil? You remember all that, Dougie?"

"Of course."

"I wonder. Been at that whore's next door."

"Only for a few minutes."

"There with that friend of yours. You should stay away from people like that, Dougie. He's bad news."

Almost instinctually, Doug wanted to defend Crank. But, after thinking about what had happened, he could only agree with Pork by nodding his head.

"That's good you're finally realizing that."

Pork crossed the room. He stood in front of Doug.

"Now we're going to use some of our senses." He leaned in until his gaping-pored nose was right in front of Dougie's mouth. "Open up. I'm a human breathalyzer. I want you to blow out. Right into my face."

"Why?"

Pork closed his eyes and shook his head. "That was all I needed. You've had at least one alcoholic beverage tonight, Dougie. And that's probably clouded your judgment. Unzip those pants."

"Why?"

"You know why. If your mother's been doing what she's supposed to, you know what's going to happen."

"I didn't do anything."

"You've already proven yourself to be a liar, Dougie. We can't have that. You're way more important to us than that."

"This is weird and it's making me feel uncomfortable."

Pork clamped a highly sensitive area between Doug's neck and shoulder. "Do it."

Doug unbuttoned and unzipped his pants. He slid them down.

"Underwear too."

Doug slid down his underwear. Pork got down on his knees, closed his eyes, and moved his nose so close it was almost touching Doug's penis. He took several deep sniffs and then stood up. Doug quickly pulled up his underwear and pants, refastening them. Pork shook his head and punched Doug in the stomach. Doug dropped to the floor.

"I smell two things on your genitals Doug. Two things that I am not supposed to smell. I smell saliva and I smell semen. You are very lucky I do not smell a woman's genital secretions. I only want to know one thing. Who?"

Doug was conflicted. He knew not answering was not an option. Pork probably wouldn't believe he had been mouth raped by an unknown assailant. If he told him the complete truth—that Mindy had rubbed herself against him until he had ejaculated and that Whitney had performed oral sex on him—that would probably also get him into more trouble.

"Whitney. The neighbor." Doug knew he probably said that because he was mad at Whitney but, to seem less petty, he told himself it was because Mindy was a member of the Church and Whitney was a heathen. Meaning Pork would see Mindy on a weekly basis but wouldn't really see Whitney unless he went out of his way to.

Why would he do that?

What would even give Doug that idea?

Could Whitney now be in danger?

That was stupid. He dismissed it.

Doug still lay on the floor. Pork bent down and lifted his head up until he was looking at the cross-shaped urn on the mantel.

"I want you to look at your dear old dad," Pork said. "Know that he's up in heaven and he is not at all happy right now. You've let him down, Dougie. Ever since Lankmeyer's unfortunate and shameful death, you are our most shining prospect. Go on up to your room now. I'm going to wait here for your mother. I hope I'm able to calm her down. I'm going to recommend that she not allow you to leave the house."

"You mean ground me?"

"If that's what you would like to call it."

"But I have a job... and driving lessons... and I'm an *adult*."

"Nope. Adults take responsibility for their actions. All you do is lie." He leveled a kick at Doug's stomach and said, "Go."

Aching, vaguely nauseous, Doug pulled himself up to his room and lay in his bed. The windows were shut and the air conditioner was running but he was pretty sure, before dozing off, he heard screams from outside. He didn't bother getting up to see who or what it was.

Thirty-nine

Crank stuck around in the woods behind Whitney's house and finished off the case. Driving the dirt bike home was a major challenge. He would have probably just walked if he didn't think Whitney, in a fit of rage, would do something to sabotage the bike. It was her first time, after all, she probably thought they were boyfriend and girlfriend now. He drove the bike into the side of the trailer and it turned itself off. When he went inside, his mother was still on the disintegrating couch watching snow on the television. He figured she must be on some kind of methamphetamine. She wasn't usually up this late unless she had a man with her.

"Stephen?" she said quietly.

"Not feelin good, Ma," he said, trying to hurry to his room.

"Stephen." More firmly this time.

"What?"

"Come here." She patted the gross cushion next to her.

"I really hafta..."

"I don't ask for much."

He slumped his shoulders and sulked over to the couch. Sat down.

With lightning quickness, his mother clenched a claw-like hand around his arm and pulled him into her. Crank smelled char or sulfur or something. His mother's eyes were fire and for a horrifying second Crank thought maybe it wasn't his mother sitting on this couch at all, but that other thing. That other thing they were supposed to talk about before Doug went apeshit.

"Stay away from Doug," his mother growled with a voice he'd never heard before. Crank tried to pull away. He was pretty sure he was going to vomit now. He was pretty sure this wasn't his mother at all, but just when he had broken his grip, her voice softened and she said, "It's just that Doug is a really good boy and wants to stay out of trouble. You don't want him to turn into this do you?"

And now Crank stood and looked at his mother from above and what he saw wasn't a human or a beast. It was more like a mummy, wasted and dry and emaciated. He charged for the bathroom and exploded into a toilet bowl filled with piss and blood.

Forty

Around dawn, Amanda made her way out of the Tabernacle, through the woods, and into town. With everything that had happened previously, she thought she should have felt weak and rubbery. But she felt just the opposite. She felt blissful. Like she floated more than walked.

When she reached her block, Officer Viled pulled up next to her in his cruiser. She stopped.

"Morning there, Miss Winthrop."

"Good morning, Officer Viled!" She couldn't stop smiling.

"You're looking very chipper and naked and covered in blood."

"Oh yes. Isn't it glorious?"

"Glory glory, Miss Winthrop. How bout you let me give you a ride home?"

"Oh, I can make it. It's just right there."

"I really should give you a ride home. What if someone sees you like that?"

"It is my natural state. Don't you think it's beautiful?"

"I definitely do, Miss Winthrop." Officer Viled licked his mustache and leered at her. "I really should give you a ride home."

She crossed the front of his car and got in the passenger seat.

He pulled into her driveway.

"I'm a witness, Officer Viled. Isn't that glorious?"

"It certainly is. What have you witnessed?"

"Magnificence."

"Does it have anything to do with the... upcoming celebration?"

"Oh yes. It has everything to do with that."

Officer Viled placed a hand on her naked, crusty thigh. "Now Miss Winthrop—"

"Please. Amanda."

"Now, Amanda, the things you witness with your, uh, *friends* should stay between you ladies, don't you think?"

"But I'm to tell the world."

He ran a hand between her legs. "You can tell the world after the Great One has come. Glory glory. We're all very excited. Until then, people might not believe you."

"They will if they look into my eyes."

"It's best not to take any chances, don't you think?"

"Maybe..."

"Let me walk you inside. Make sure you get there safely."

"But it's just right there."

Officer Viled's good natured expression dropped. "Miss Winthrop. Amanda. I'm going to take you inside and fuck you. I think you'll like it. I'll use my gun and everything. And then you can get some rest so you can be a refreshed little witness for the rest of the week. What do you say to that?"

"But we are now reserved for the Great Lord."

"Not you, Amanda. Only them. The other girls. You're a witness, remember? You can still fuck whoever you want. You do want to, don't you?"

"Of course. And you're sure nothing will happen?"

"As long as you have eyes in your head and a pretty little mouth to tell the world what you seen, you'll be just fine."

She was already out of the car, Officer Viled behind her, watching her ass, his erection straining against his trousers.

Forty-one

Doug called in sick at America Pantry. Patel called him a dog fucker and said he was calling Crank. Patel called back a few minutes later and told Doug that Crank thought he was dying. Patel referred to him as a little girl. Doug said he still couldn't come in. Patel accused him of staying home to fuck six dogs and hung up.

Doug felt dirty and took three showers. Otherwise he didn't leave his room. Not to eat. Not to drink. And not to use the restroom. He thought it seemed like something a monk or a priest would do. He had a lot of thinking to do. Mindy called late in the afternoon to tell him she wouldn't be able to give him any more driving lessons until after her party Friday. She told him she didn't like what they had done the other day and wanted him to know she would love to be his girlfriend and would he wait for her? Would he not mess around with any skanky girls that might live in the neighborhood, despite the accessibility and temptation? Doug assured her she was safe. He told her he was no longer friends with Crank or Whitney, which was good because now he didn't have to feel guilty about coming to her party on Friday. She said she thought that was really good for everyone and then hung up after saying she loved him. Doug was stunned. Something else to think about.

That night Mindy and the other girls stole a young Mexican girl from a mall outside Cincinnati. They brought her back to the Tabernacle, skinned her alive, and danced in her blood. There were also three goats involved. They had wanted four but the man from Baal's told her they were on backorder.

The beast rested, waiting for Friday.

Wednesday, June 18th

Forty-two

Doug awoke to his mom poking him in the cheek with the phone.

"Quit it." He batted at the phone.

"It's the Pantry."

"I don't work today."

"It's the Pantry. Besides, it's time you got up. It's almost noon."

It was really great his boss was hearing this. So not only did he live with his mother, she also had to wake him up.

Doug took the phone and said, "Hello?"

"Good morning, Momma's boy. I need you to come in today."

"But I'm off." He really didn't want to go into today. He didn't have much else to do except for church in the evening but... he just didn't feel comfortable leaving the house. Too much temptation. Too much vile filth. Especially at a place that seemed to cater to vice. "I have... plans."

Patel laughed. "Soon you will have plans but no money. Then no plans."

"Look, I've come in a lot when you've asked me on my days off. I just can't today, okay? Have you tried Crank?"

"Crank quit. He is dog shit with worms."

This kind of surprised Doug. America Pantry was a slacker's paradise. Not to mention all the booze, condoms, cigarettes and, apparently, Duraflames Crank could ever need. He had often imagined Crank retiring from the Pantry.

"Well, I'm very sorry. I'll be there tomorrow."

"You are a lazy skank."

Doug tried to protest but Patel had already hung up.

His mother still stood there. Now she held her hand out for the phone. As soon as she closed her meaty hand around it, it rang again. She looked at the number on the caller ID and shook her head, meaning she didn't recognize it. Meaning she wasn't just going to hand the phone over to him.

"Hello?" she said. Then handed the phone to him and said, "It's a girl for you."

Doug got excited. It was probably Mindy. Maybe just calling to talk. He took the phone and waited for his mother to leave, but she didn't. She pulled a cigarette from her housecoat and lit up, saying, "I know what you've been up to. I'm standing right here."

"Hello," Doug said.

"Hi Doug. It's Whitney. Listen—"

He hung up and handed the phone back to his mother. "Block that number."

"Who was it?"

"The Devil."

"Who did you think it was?"

"It's not important."

His mother ashed into his trashcan and sat down on his bed. He rolled over and faced the wall, pulling the covers over his head.

"I know you're eighteen, an adult, and you're going to start dating girls. But if you want me to be okay with who you're dating, I have to approve of them. If you're waiting for that *whore* next door to call, then that's a problem. She's crazy. You know where she's been the past few years, don't you? I can't believe you'd let yourself get mixed up with trash like that."

"That's who it was. I don't want anything to do with her. She doesn't have any morals. I'm dating Mindy Astan. You know her, don't you? She goes to the Church. Or the Tabernacle, anyway."

"Oh." His mother sounded surprised. "That's a good find, Dougie. I hope it works out."

There was something about this calm acceptance Doug couldn't believe. "She's graduating from the Tabernacle, you know." He pulled the blanket off his head and sat up against the headboard. "There's a graduation party on Friday."

"Oh, it's more than that. It's the graduation ceremony. Those three girls have worked very hard. I'll be there. The whole church will be there. Which reminds me... there isn't any church tonight. They're preparing things. I wasn't going to tell you because I didn't want you making any plans. It's a shame though. I think church is *exactly* where you need to be."

"No plans. We weren't planning on seeing each other until after the ceremony. We thought that would be best."

"So now what are you going to do with your day?"

"I'm just going to stick around. Maybe go for a walk. Think about my relationship with God."

She patted him on the calf. "You're such a good boy, Dougie. I know you've made some mistakes the past few days but hormones are funny things. I think you'll find the light again."

"I'm trying."

She stood up and left the room in a cloud of smoke.

Forty-three

Crank woke up sometime that afternoon. He'd lodged a chair under the handle of the door in case his mother tried to murder him in his sleep. It was probably more symbolic than anything since everything in the trailer was made so cheaply a toddler could break it. The chair under the knob was probably stronger than the door itself. But since he woke up and wasn't covered in blood, it seemed everything had worked out. He called his band mates to arrange a last minute practice session. He wanted to be around as many people as possible and he didn't want any of those people to be Doug. He thought about calling Whitney and decided not to. She was kind of a bummer. And she wouldn't want to talk about anything except the Doug situation. Which was exactly not how Crank liked to deal with things. He would prefer to forget about it and put it off as long as possible, hoping the problem would pass. That required less effort and usually worked out.

When Lurk, Patrick Crayze, and a couple of really high girls showed up, Crank sent Lurk out to make some fliers and post them around town. He never came back and that didn't surprise Crank at all, since he was kind of shocked Lurk had been conscious when he showed up. They continued with the band practice anyway. Lurk wasn't completely central to their sound. The girls took off their clothes and danced around. Crank's mom showed up just before dusk, hopped up on something, and proceeded to take laps around the trailer, her eyes bugging out, her starched hair clumping out behind her head. Crank was worried she might have a heart attack but when she got tired she went inside and fell asleep on the couch.

After Patrick Crayze and the girls went home, Crank called Amber and told her he was sleeping in a tent in her back yard. She said her parents were out of town so he could sleep in the house. So he brought his tent and set it up in the living room.

Forty-four

Doug took a scalding shower and put on clean clothes. He took the clothes he wore yesterday and put them into a trash bag. He turned on his computer and restored it to its factory condition. He no longer had any use for it. He unhooked it from the wall and put it in the trash bag with the clothes. He dusted the computer desk and put his Bible on it. He took the trash bag downstairs and put it in front of his mother, who was on the couch cutting her thick yellow toenails, a cigarette dangling from her mouth.

"I'd like you to burn the clothes and donate the computer to the thrift store."

"Aren't you going to need it?"

"If I need one, I can go to the library. I'd prefer not to have it in my room."

"It would help with college if you decide to go."

"It's like having a den of sin in my room, Mom. No good Christian should have one of these in his home. Especially not if it's connected to the Internet." Then he pointed at the television, which was on. "Or one of those."

"I'm not getting rid of my TV."

"Use it responsibly." Doug went back up to his room. It seemed lighter and airier. Roomier. More pure.

He lay on his bed and crossed his hands over his chest.

Tomorrow he would go to work and give Patel his two weeks' notice. He would call around town looking for another job. Working at the library would be pretty cool, he thought, except it would be kind of the same thing as working at Patel's because he would be renting them smut for their minds, instead of their bodies. And they wouldn't even be paying for it. So that was out. He could work for the Church but he didn't think he could take any money for that. Maybe he could see if Pastor Don owned any more businesses in town. At least then, he would know his work was for a decent and God-fearing person. He could work at the cemetery digging graves or something. It would be grim but it was all a part of life and it *did* have a spiritual element to it.

He would just have to wait and see. God would provide.

Besides his mother, there were really only three other people he dealt with on a social basis: Crank, Mindy, and Whitney. Clover was a small town. He wasn't self-delusional enough to think he could go the rest of his life without seeing Crank and Whitney. Mindy, he couldn't wait to finally see at her ceremony. He tried not to think of her so it would be even more special when he finally *did* get to see her. Crank and Whitney were a different matter altogether. Doug knew he had a tendency to be spiteful and he knew that was probably wrong. Although he personally didn't see anything wrong with it if the spite's intention was to keep his spiritual well-being intact. Regardless, he could not let that spite blossom into hate. Therefore, when he ran into either of them again (it was inevitable, especially while he continued to work at the Pantry), he needed to nip the relationships in the bud before they became something more menacing. Besides being neighbors and his brief lapse in moral judgment, he wasn't that really close to Whitney. Despite her willingness to take his penis into her mouth and do even more if he had been able, she didn't seem to really like him very much. So he thought if he told her it was best they didn't really talk or "hang out" anymore, she would understand. She would probably be angry. She seemed angry a lot. He would just have to tell her he was involved with another woman and definitely could no longer do anything like they had again. Maybe he could tell her if she wanted to become a churchgoer they could continue to talk so long as they were talking about God and Jesus and good things that strengthened the moral fiber. Wholesome activities. Crank was a slightly different matter. He had been friends with Crank for a long time but they had... grown apart. That's really all it came down to. Crank was a twelve-year-old boy with the freedoms and physicality of an adult. Doug hoped Crank was capable of good things but he didn't think they could be friends until Crank decided to respect Doug and maybe, well, *grow up* a little bit. Crank wouldn't like to hear that but he didn't get mad very easily and despite his eagerness to offend Doug at every chance, he *did* respect Doug to a certain extent. Maybe he realized Doug was more grown up, more *adult* than he was. In the end, Doug didn't really look forward to either of these encounters but he knew he had the strength to deal with them. And that was something.

Doug closed his eyes and took several deep even breaths. He felt a calm and peaceful easiness spread out from his chest completely unlike the spinning chaos he'd felt the couple times he'd gone to bed with his head full of drink. Drifting off, he had the sense his body and his spirit were healing, becoming not only what they were but something even more connected and complete. He dreamed of blue skies and clouds, running streams and clear sunlight.

Forty-five

Mindy was furious. "What do you mean you don't have any?"

"Just what I said. Y'all done run us out," the man from Baal's said on the other end of the line.

"Well where else are we going to get a fucking goat?"

"Probably nowhere this hour."

"We need something living."

"Look, I don't know what y'all are doin up there but whatever it is I'm sure it can wait."

"What we're doing isn't any of your business. What else can you bring us?"

"Beg your pardon?"

"What else can you bring us? Do you just deliver goats? I'm sure you can get something else."

"I'm starting to feel uncomfortable."

"We pay you don't we?"

"The Church pays me. I'm assuming whatever you're doing is for a good cause."

"That's exactly right. A very good cause. The whole town's well-being hinges on it. So you'd better bring us something. I'll make it very worth your while."

There was a pause on the other end of the line.

"*Hello?*"

"It might take a little longer."

"I'm not going to ask any questions. Just so long as we have something before dawn. Think you can manage that?"

"Doesn't sound like I have much of a choice. Where am I taking it?"

"The Tabernacle."

"Someone'll be there?"

"Yes."

"Okay."

Mindy angrily poked her phone off.

"Well?" Kristen said.

"He's bringing *some*thing."

"I guess we'd better get out there, huh? Are we picking up the crazy bitch?"

"I can live without it."

"I do enjoy her sexual energy."

"Fine. We'll vote. Angie?"

"I thought the sex stuff was over anyway."

"We're just not allowed to fuck anything with a cock," Mindy said.

"Sure," Angie said. "We can swing by her house. Foursies is better than threesies."

Mindy rolled her eyes. "Let's go then."

They headed out and hopped in Kristen's red convertible and drove to Amanda's. They pulled into her driveway and Mindy said, "I'm not going to get her."

"You're *such* a brat," Kristen said, sliding out from behind the wheel and walking to Amanda's door. She didn't see any lights on but rang the bell. After a few minutes Officer Viled opened the door. He was completely naked, his chest covered in deep red welts. He smelled heavily of sex. He absently stroked himself and stared at Kristen.

"Officer Viled?"

"I'm off duty."

"Is Amanda around?"

"She's resting up."

Kristen wasn't expecting this. She thought Amanda would answer the door and come with them with the same eager zeal she had in the past. "Okay, well, if she wakes up can you tell her that we'll be at the Tabernacle if she wants to meet us there."

Officer Viled glanced over Kristen's shoulder at the two other girls in the car. "You girls are welcome to bring the party here if that's what you were planning on doing."

"I'm sorry. We really have to be at the Tabernacle. It's church stuff."

"I see." He turned away absently and shut the door.

Kristen shrugged and went back to the car. "No Amanda," she said.

"Was that—?"

"Office Viled. What a creep."

Kristen peeled out of the driveway and gunned the car through the neighborhood. She cranked the stereo. She had a great recording of Charlton Heston reading the Bible backmasked, with synth music and a drumbeat. The band was called, appropriately, Fucking Heston's Corpse, and it was one of her current favorites. The other girls didn't complain. It only took about ten minutes to get to the Tabernacle. They threw open the door and the pungent smell of death wafted out.

"I think I'm going to be sick," Angie said.

"You are not going to be sick," Mindy said. "That is the sweet smell of sacrifice."

"There's nothing sweet about it."

"You just earned ten lashes."

Angie stuck out her bottom lip in a pout. They entered the Tabernacle, its walls and floor slathered with the congealing mess of their previous sacrifices. There were now maggots and flies everywhere. Mindy, for one, was grateful Pastor Don had allowed them to move things to the Tabernacle. Cleaning up the house had been a bitch. Of course she realized that Pastor Don only acted on orders from that higher power. Unfortunately they wouldn't see him until the ceremony on Friday. Mindy couldn't wait. He would be so happy to see the work they had done.

"Kristen, you light the candles. I'll take care of Angie's punishment."

Kristen went about lighting the candles. Mindy told Angie to take off her clothes, which she did obediently.

"Now put your hands against the wall."

Angie put her hands against the wall and stuck out her ass. Mindy didn't have a whip so she smacked her ten times, five on each cheek, until her hand stung as badly as Angie's red ass probably did. When the man from Baal's finally got there, Mindy made Angie answer the door naked.

Angie pulled the door open. Kristen and Mindy stood farther back in the room, giggling and blood thirsty. Angie did her best to cover herself. The man from Baal's made no attempt to look away. In his hands he held a chicken, proffering it forward for Angie to take. Mindy's laughs turned into immediate rage as she stormed across the room, standing between Angie and the deliveryman.

"Enjoy the show?" she said.

"Huh?"

"That was probably more skin than you've seen in the last ten years." Mindy poked the chicken's head and said, "What the hell is this?"

"It's a chicken."

"Yes, but why are you standing there holding it with that stupid look on your face?"

"It's the only thing I could get."

"This isn't acceptable."

"You asked for anything."

"Yes, but... Oh shit. Step in for a minute."

The man rumpled his nose. "I think I'm fine out here."

Mindy turned toward Angie. "Take your hands away. If he tries to look around them any harder he's going to have a heart attack."

Angie took her hands away from her breasts and in front of her crotch and let them hang by her sides.

The deliveryman continued to hold the chicken and stare stupidly at her, as though he wasn't in the midst of an argument. Now Mindy put her hand on his shoulder and coaxed him inside. With Angie in her current state, it wasn't very hard.

"Just come in and give me a second to figure something out."

Mindy moved between him and the door.

"Angie," Mindy said. "Service this man while I think of something else to do. This chicken isn't going to work."

Angie moved forward. Mindy heard the man gulp.

"You can put down the chicken."

He put down the chicken. Angie dropped to her knees in front of him and unzipped his pants. The man was hugely erect. Probably had been since he'd received the call from Mindy. Angie wrapped her hand around the base of his shaft and almost took it into her mouth before stopping and saying, "I didn't think we were supposed to do this. Only with each other. Right? Isn't that what you said?"

"You don't have to fuck him," Mindy said. "Just blow him and let him come on your tits or something."

Angie took him into her mouth, slowly working her lips down the length of the deliveryman's shaft. Mindy picked up the sacrificial knife. She could have picked up an active tornado siren and the deliveryman wouldn't have noticed. She crossed the room to where Angie had him in her mouth, quickly and deftly wrapped her free arm around his chest and upper arms, and sliced with the hand holding the sacrificial knife. A fount of blood shot across the room and drenched Angie's back and the top of her head. Mindy stood out of the way and allowed the deliveryman to fall to the floor. Angie stood up, gagging. She coughed and said, "Oh, the fucker shot in my mouth."

"Grow up," Mindy said, letting the knife clatter onto the floor.

The man's legs spasmed and the other two girls disrobed before moving in to bathe in the last of his dying blood.

The chicken stood in the corner, horrified, until later when the girls closed in on it too.

Thursday June 19th

Forty-six

Doug gathered the tracts and put them into a large paper grocery bag. He didn't even know if there were this many people in Clover. Not that he would have the time to visit every house. But it was best to be prepared. And some of the people he visited would probably want pamphlets to give to their friends. He thought this would be a good exercise. So busy with his senior year of high school and graduation, he hadn't done this in over a year. Someone at the Church should have put some pressure on him. Since working at America Pantry, his only experience with the people of Clover was to sell them things that would either rot their bodies or the environment.

As he crossed the living room to the front door his mom asked, "What are you doing?"

"I'm going visiting." The explanation was very easy and only took a second. Yet this was the kind of response he would have felt exhausted to give and even gone out of his way to avoid only a couple of days before.

"Visiting?"

"Yeah, handing out the tracts like we used to. Want to come along?"

"Maybe you should just stay home."

"No. I think I need to do this. Really, come along."

"I've got my shows."

"DVR them. Are your shows more important than your god?"

"You sure are a good kid, Dougie."

"*Man*. I'm a man now."

A momentary look of horror crossed his mother's face and it took Doug a second to realize why.

He laughed and said, "I don't mean like that. Not until I'm married. But I am eighteen and therefore have a man's responsibilities. So what do you think? Coming along?"

She sighed. "I was really hoping to stay inside in the air conditioning today, but if you're going to try and make me feel guilty about it..."

She stood up and motioned to her muumuu and slippers. "I guess what I have on is fine."

"No reason for vanity amongst neighbors."

They walked outside and Doug's mom went to the car. Doug was already nearly at the sidewalk.

"Aren't we walking?"

"You can do the walking. I'll follow behind you in the car. It's hot out here and I'm in no shape to walk all up and down the neighborhood."

Doug wanted to say how he thought that kind of defeated the purpose of "visiting". Maybe if someone invited him in, she would get out of the car and follow him. Who was he to judge?

As he turned in the opposite direction of Whitney's and began walking down the sidewalk, he could almost swear he saw Deacon Pork's Cadillac cruise slowly through the intersection. He went up the walk to Mrs. Sinkwater's house and rang the bell. While he waited for someone to either come to the door or hide inside, he pulled a tract from his bag.

The door opened and Mrs. Sinkwater stood there, batting her eyelashes at him. She was probably older than his mother.

"Oh, hello, Doug!" She reached out and patted him gingerly on the shoulder. "Please come in."

She practically yanked him into the house. Now she was very close to him, rubbing her hands on his chest, her face only a couple of inches from his. He could smell the Listerine covering the halitosis reek coming from her mouth. She was making him very uncomfortable.

"To what do I owe this surprise to?"

"I don't..."

The front door opened and his mother filled the doorway.

Mrs. Sinkwater quickly backed away from Doug. "Well, hi, Martha, I didn't realize you were with Doug today."

"Just makin the rounds like old times. Doin some visiting, you know?"

Mrs. Sinkwater took the tract from Doug's hand. Doug went through his spiel and then Mrs. Sinkwater and his mom spent about ten minutes talking. They left to go to the next house but Doug still felt odd about the scene at Mrs. Sinkwater's. He felt violated.

Halfway to the next house, Doug heard from behind him, "Doug. Doug. Doug. Doug."

He turned to look.

It was Whitney.

"I really need to talk to you."

Doug motioned toward his mother, as though she could be missed. Regardless, he didn't want to talk to Whitney. Before she could say anything, his mother advanced on her. The look in Whitney's eyes was both defiant and fearful.

"You think I don't know what you've been up to," his mom said.

"I'm sorry, Mrs. Backus, but this is very important."

Doug's mom slapped Whitney in the face. Whitney tried to push her but she stood, stout and immovable. Doug's mom punched Whitney in the stomach, dropping her to the ground.

Doug wondered if he should defend her but he didn't feel like it. Suddenly he didn't feel like doing much of anything. His mother continued to pound on Whitney. It looked like Whitney had already gotten in a fight and Doug wondered about that, but only briefly. He was appalled at his mother's unchristian conduct. He dropped the bag of tracts and said, "I'm going home."

He walked past Whitney and his mother brawling in the sidewalk.

He went into his house and up to his room.

He slammed the door shut and thought something really needed to be done.

Forty-seven

Crank lay on his bed, staring up at the ceiling. Something slammed into his door, trying to open it. It was a good thing he'd remembered to put the chair there. The door bulged again. It probably wouldn't take much to bust the door around the chair, but he didn't think his mother had the power to do it and that was who he was worried about the most.

"You're not getting in, bitch!" He lit a cigarette, figuring he could burn her in the eye or something if she actually managed to make it in.

"Which bitch are you talking about?" a voice significantly younger than his mother's said.

"Is my mom out there?"

"I didn't see her. Are you going to open the door?"

"Chloe?"

"No, douche, it's Whitney."

"You weren't able to talk to Doug?"

"No. Will you open the fucking door?"

Crank got off the bed and removed the chair from under the door's knob. The door opened and a battered looking Whitney stood there.

"What the fuck happened to you?"

"First that fat fuck Pork happened to me—"

"The guy who dresses like a wrestler?"

"Yeah. He must have somehow found out about what happened between me and Doug. It was a warning but it really just showed how serious things are and how right I am about what I thought was going on."

Crank stared off into some middle distance behind Whitney and said, "And then?"

"And then today I found Doug and his mom out walking in the neighborhood and when I tried to talk to him, *she* beat me up."

"She's a large woman. Built like a man."

"Fights like a man."

"It's kind of hot. The bruises and shit."

"You sick fuck."

But Crank's hands were already on her shoulders, dragging her into the room. She tried to resist even as he slid a hand up the inside of her leg, lifting her dress.

"No. Huh-uh." She tried to brush his hand away.

"If you want me to keep listening to you and help and all that..."

"Jesus, you're even lazy when it comes to blackmail."

He bent her over the bed, pulled her underwear down her legs and got on his knees behind her. He gruffly spread her ass cheeks and started tonguing her asshole and cunt. He took his head away to say, "You can still talk. I'm listening."

"And you'll help?"

"Depends on what it is."

"If you think you're putting that diseased dick in me before agreeing then I *could* just leave now."

"Fine, I'll help. Have you come yet?"

"No. Keep going. I'm close. And thanks. That feels nice."

"No problem."

Amidst Crank's slurping, Whitney told him what they needed to do. He said he had the show tomorrow and she told him as long as he was finished a little before midnight it wouldn't matter. While Crank had her on her hands and knees on the bed, going at her from behind, his mother came home. She seemed happy with the situation more so than angered. Crank didn't stop and Whitney thought it would almost be more awkward to stop and acknowledge the woman's presence than to just pretend she hadn't noticed her come in. Crank's mom stood there for a while before finally going to pass out on the couch, the television turned to top volume, her hand down the front of her pants.

Forty-eight

The beast rested, thinking about tomorrow at the stroke of midnight, just as the twentieth became the twenty-first. It would drink the blood of the virgin, the sacrifice, and its nights of rest would all be worth it.

Forty-nine

When Whitney left Crank's trailer, she felt slightly better about things. She had considered asking him to walk her home but figured, if need be, she stood a better chance at surviving things alone. Her brief period of guilt about letting Crank take her virginity had ended tonight as Crank fucked her for what felt like hours. She knew about Crank, knew he would never consider them boyfriend and girlfriend. And that wasn't something she wanted anyway. There weren't many men or even boys in Clover and, at first, as much as she hated to admit it, she was planning on helping Doug because she was attracted to him. Now she felt like that probably wasn't an option but she was going to try and help him anyway. It made her feel like she was doing a good thing.

Altruism.

That was the word she was trying to think of.

Walking the back country roads through the hills and, later, the town, was uneventful save for the buzzing energy around her. It made her think of the heightened electricity in the air before a storm.

Fifty

Officer Viled had had Amanda handcuffed to the bed for she didn't know how long. Part of her thought he was trying to keep her from getting out but parts of *him* delivered such exquisite pleasure to her that she quickly put those thoughts out of her head. He was the Law. If he told her to do something then she was going to do it. The Church was another kind of law, and when it had told her to open her eyes and witness, she had done that as well.

Things were so much different since Perry had died.

So much better.

Friday, June 20th

Fifty-one

When Doug got to America Pantry for what he had decided would be his final day of work, he was surprised to find no one there. The door was unlocked, but there was no sign of Patel or even Crank. Then he remembered Crank had quit. That made Doug feel even worse about not even giving Patel two weeks' notice.

On the ride over, his mother had seemed groggy and ill-tempered.

He spent the morning searching the paper for apartments. The only affordable places were trailers. If it weren't for his close affiliation with the Church, he would leave Clover altogether. Then he thought of people like Whitney and Crank, the diseases this town put in its children, and thought this town needed him.

He smelled perfume and looked up to see a moderately attractive woman standing at the counter. He must have been off in his own little world. He hadn't even heard her come in. He started to ring her up before realizing she hadn't put anything on the counter.

"Can I help you?" he said.

"I need it," she practically moaned.

"Need what?"

She slid a hand down the front of her jeans.

"You know," she said.

Doug backed away. Why was this happening to him?

She started to come around the counter and the door jingled. Deacon Pork stormed to the woman and grabbed her roughly around the arm.

"Maybe you should go home, Mrs. Pauley," he said, leading her to the front door.

The phone rang. Doug picked it up.

"America Pantry."

"Doug..."

He slammed the phone down. It was Whitney. Maybe when things were calmer, he could talk to her, he could try and bring her to the light, but not now.

Deacon Pork stood on the other side of the counter.

"I think maybe I'd better hang around here with you all day. What with the trust issues and everything."

Doug didn't know what to say. This was one of his teachers, one of his leaders, and he had let him down. As much as he wanted to tell Pork he didn't need the control, he knew Pork wouldn't see it that way.

"Um... okay." He didn't know what else he could say.

Pork parked himself in the back of the store, his arms crossed over his wide barrel chest, looking like the most conspicuous security guard in the world. He stared continually at Doug. After a few minutes, Doug stopped being nervous. Most of the customers were like the first of the day. Doug began to wonder if he was exuding pheromones or something.

He didn't see how he could go eighteen years of his life without any interest from the opposite sex and then have this much attention bestowed upon him in only a week or two.

It was strange.

It was all a test of faith.

Besides, if he had received attention from girls earlier on, there was a really good chance he never would have found the Church.

Each time he was approached, Pork was immediately at the

counter to pull the offending female toward the door.

Sometime after noon, Whitney came to the store. She didn't even make it to the counter. As soon as she spotted Pork, she turned and left.

Maybe he should have answered her call.

Nah. If it was important, she'd call back.

After fending off a few more women, the phone rang.

It was Whitney. "Don't hang up!" she said.

He was wrong. He definitely didn't want to talk to her. Just the sound of her voice brought back all the anger. He didn't like feeling angry.

"I have really important things to say!"

Then, as the phone was on its way to the cradle, he heard her yell, "Don't go tonight! ... Dad's urn!"

He almost wanted to snatch the phone up and shout, "What about my dad's urn?!" but felt like that would give her too much satisfaction. She was probably just saying things that would pique his interest.

Lies.

He looked at Pork and shouted, "Lies!"

Pork nodded his head like he understood.

Fifty-two

Crank was in the bathroom with his shirt off, flexing in front of the mirror when Whitney knocked on the bathroom door.

"He wouldn't talk to me," she said. "And my pussy really hurts."

"Probably just a UTI."

"You're going to have to try talking to him."

Crank opened the door. "Can't do that."

"Because of your stupid show?"

"Yeah, this is a big one."

"What... twelve, thirteen people?"

"Tons."

"Tons of fat people is only like seven or eight."

"And we got some Duraflames."

"What the fuck are those?"

"Pyrotechnics."

"Okay. Well, tell yourself that when your best friend gets sacrificed to the dark lord."

Crank scoffed. "All that stuff is shit."

"How can you still believe that after everything I've told you?"

"Girls lie. About everything."

"But you're still coming after the show, right?"

"To the Church? Yeah, I'll be there."

"By midnight?"

"By midnight. Hey, wanna give me a blowjob?"

"Not particularly."

"I just figured... since your pussy was sore and shit."

Whitney snatched out her hand and punched Crank in the crotch. "And you're *still* going to help me, bitch."

Fifty-three

By early afternoon, probably the fifteenth woman threw herself at Doug. And not all of them had been women. A couple of them were probably elementary school kids. Pork had apparently had enough.

"I've called your mother," Pork said. "She's on her way to pick you up."

"But I'm here until five."

"No, you're going with your mother. See you at the ceremony tonight."

"But I need to talk to Patel."

"I'll punch you in the face if you don't go with your mother. She's here now."

Doug slumped his shoulders and walked out as his mother pulled up into the parking lot. He opened the back door and slid into the back seat.

"What are you doing?" his mother asked.

"Avoiding as much cigarette smoke as I can."

"You're being a little ass is what you're doing."

"Do we have to do this now?"

"You're the one who sat in the back."

"You're the one who developed a smoking habit."

His mom tossed her cigarette out the window, rolled it up, and exhaled.

"Now I'm not smoking," she said.

Doug pulled his shirt up over his head.

Fifty-four

After coming on her face and wiping his penis off in her hair, Officer Viled undid Amanda's handcuffs and told her to go take a shower. "You smell like a whore's mattress."

She felt sore inside and out, but this pain created a type of ecstatic lightness within her. She wondered what Officer Viled had planned for her. Then he was in the shower with her. It was like just thinking about him made him appear.

"I had to trim my mustache," he said.

"It looks great," she said. And it did. "So what are we doing tonight?"

"What... you think I have plans for us just because I asked you to take a shower?"

"I guess we don't have to."

He vigorously tugged his penis. "Seems like you've been perfectly happy right here the past couple of days."

"I told you we don't have to."

"Have you forgotten already?"

"Forgotten?"

"The ceremony. What you were called to witness on."

Amanda couldn't remember if she was called upon to witness anything specifically or not. So far it seemed like she had witnessed a lot of things. Some of them were awful, but awful in a beautiful way.

Officer Viled breathed out harshly. "The final appearance of Our Lord."

"The Beast?"

"Yes! And you are to witness it and then go out into the world to tell people about it."

She still wasn't grasping the exact details but she thought it sounded good anyway. "Yes," she said. "That sounds glorious."

"Glorious! Of course. Glory glory."

Amanda grew excited and asked him if he wanted to make love. He said his penis was too raw. She told him she couldn't wait for tonight. When she got out of the shower, she put on the last nice dress she had, pounded a bottle of wine, and collapsed on the couch, waiting for Officer Viled to take her to the Church.

Fifty-five

To anyone else, the Tabernacle would have smelled toxic. To the three initiates, it smelled like a labor of love. All of their recent sacrifices now covered this room. Maggots writhed in the decaying corpses. The flies clouded the small space. And they themselves were covered in this same rot. It seemed like such a shame to wash it off. But that's what they were supposed to do. What they'd been doing to the Tabernacle was creating a domicile for their Lord to return to. What they'd been doing with themselves was training to provide them with the skills that would please their Lord.

In the afternoon sunlight, the three girls went down to the river and laid their clothes on the bank before wading into the water. With flowered soap, they washed every surface of their bodies. And with the sacrificial knife, they shaved all of their hair. When there was blood, they greedily lapped at it, thirsting for more. But they would get more tonight. And it would be the purest kind.

Fifty-six

"Just keep piling them back there," Crank said.

Patrick Crayze kept kicking the individually packaged logs from the bed of the truck. Lurk stayed in the cab, his head lolling on the seat. It didn't strike any of them as absurd that Crank was giving them the directions. Once all the logs were in place, loosely scattered toward the back of the cave, they decided they needed to rehearse so they went back to Crank's to gather the instruments and the few remaining logs. They went through the drive-thru downtown and bought two cases of beer from the albino girl with the pegleg who would sell beer to anyone in a car.

By the time they got back to the cave, they decided they didn't really need to rehearse. Plugging in their instruments would be enough. They couldn't find any plugs and Crank started to wonder about the house lights. He knew he'd been to see shows here before. He knew there had been stage lights and amplified sound. No pyrotechnics, but the essentials. That's why he thought the pyrotechnics would blow them away. If it was a group of people standing around and listening to acoustic music coming from a band they couldn't see... he didn't know.

Maybe that would make the pyrotechnics even more awesome. More extreme.

Fifty-seven

Doug wanted to look in the urn but then his mother would ask him why he was looking in the urn. Maybe he should just do it. Maybe then they could finally have it out. But there seemed to be something so disrespectful about it. If it didn't involve his dead father...

He looked toward the urn.

It wasn't there.

Now he felt like he should be the one confronting his mother.

She trundled up behind him.

"Where's Dad?"

"Huh?" She already had another cigarette in her mouth.

"The *urn*? Where is it?"

"I took it into the kitchen to clean it. You know you gotta use that stainless steel junk on..."

Doug turned toward the kitchen.

"You don't need to go in there."

"I want to see it."

She grabbed his arm. He shook it off, went to the kitchen, opened the door, didn't see any sign of the urn.

"Where is it again?"

"I..."

"Why are you lying to me?"

"Well, I had an... accident while I was cleaning it."

"An accident."

"I dropped it."

"And?"

"All the ashes fell out."

"*All* of them!"

"Well, you know, the ones that weren't scattered over the baseball field."

"Okay. Show them to me."

"Show them to you?"

"Yeah. If you spilled them then either you left them lie there or you cleaned them up. If you cleaned them up then they must be in the garbage can or something."

"I... I put them in the ashtray."

"Show me."

She began leading him into the living room before stopping.

"Okay. Okay," she said. "It wasn't today that it happened. Is that what you wanted to hear?"

Doug didn't really know how to answer her. He didn't know what he wanted to hear. His head began spinning. "I..." He stumbled to the couch and sat down heavily. "I just want to hear that I had a dad."

The weight of that truth struck him.

"Will you please let me see the urn?"

His mother left the room. Not in the direction of the kitchen. In the direction of the garage. So it was either in the garage or in the attic. Definitely well out of sight. Maybe she was hoping someone would steal it.

But why today?

Was it because they had been fighting so much? Was it her passive aggressive way of sending a signal to him?

Something else occurred to him.

She was finally going to come clean. Doug felt the dreaded truth was that she didn't know who the father was. Or knew who the father was but didn't know where he was.

It made perfect sense.

Died before Doug was actually born? Who does that actually happen to?

Maybe she got pregnant and never even told the father. Maybe she just wanted a child and didn't really care who the father was.

Doug didn't know how he felt about the thought of his father being out there.

Would he try to find him if he was? Probably not.

But wasn't it more uplifting to think the person who contributed to his life was still alive and not dead, not lying half-scattered over some high school baseball field and half-scattered in one of his mom's ashtrays? Both of those places seemed depressing.

And that was another thing... If his father had been such a great athlete, why hadn't Doug inherited any of those traits?

His mother fatted down on the couch next to him, holding the urn in the lap of her dress.

Doug lifted off the top of it and looked inside. It was too dark to see anything. He stuck his finger in and rubbed the residue. Smelled it. Cigarette ash.

He nearly shook with anger.

"This is cigarette ash."

His mother nearly laughed. Doug stood quickly from the couch. "How dare you laugh at me! After lying to me all these years!"

"I don't know what you mean. You can't tell the difference between ashes. That's ridiculous."

"Stop calling me ridiculous!"

Doug grabbed the heavy urn. It was like something else flooded into his body. Some emptiness like the inside of the urn. The metal was cool in his palms. He lifted it above his head. A brief look of fear flickered in his mother's eyes but she still had that stupid chuckling smile on her lips.

"Stop laughing at me!"

He brought the urn down on one of her beefy shoulders. Hard, but not hard enough to justify her response.

She screamed. She threw herself onto the floor, knocking the coffee table over onto its side. She flopped around and then lay very still like Doug had killed her or something.

And though he was absolutely sure that wasn't the case, he still felt nervous. Nervous enough to want to get out and nervous enough to want to make sure she was okay. He bent down and checked the pulse on her wrist. He had to dig hard to find it but it was there, thudding away as much as the heart of a morbidly obese smoker who never moves ever does.

Doug rested the cross-shaped urn on his shoulder and made his way to the front door.

Fifty-eight

Whitney didn't know what else to do so she walked to the Ark Sakura. This walking everywhere bullshit was getting exhausting. The bank people had come to repossess her mother's car the day after Whitney had taken Doug home from Crank's. It took nearly two hours and she was covered in sweat. She wasn't even wearing her cardigan. She really needed a car. As soon as she got out of Clover, that would be her first priority. Well, her first priority would be finding a place to stay. And then probably a job. But a car was definitely up there. Or maybe just finding a friend with a car. Or just a friend who wasn't either a Bible thumping juvenile or a sex obsessed retard.

The sun was low by the time she got there. She expected to see people milling about but she didn't see anything except the dark mouth of the cave.

"Crank?" she called. She didn't remember the other guys' names and didn't really think they were functional enough to answer her anyway. Normally going into the cave wouldn't have frightened her but, given the two beatings she had received lately and the overall psychotic atmosphere of the town, she wasn't about to go into a dark, probably claustrophobic area with no rear exit.

She turned and left, guessing she would just go back home and wait for Doug. Maybe he'd done what she told him to do and checked the urn. She hoped he had come to some conclusions. She hoped she would be able to get him alone for a minute or two. She hoped she could make him believe her but wasn't sure that was possible.

Whitney figured all men were governed by the vagina. Whatever the man's actual beliefs were, if he was heterosexual, the vagina was his one true god. He either wanted a lot of it or one secure vagina. Like investments. When you went for one vagina, made yourself stable and righteous, that was security. Each man could take his pick. Few opted out by choice and she figured those guys were just confused.

She pegged Doug as a secure investment type of guy. Forty-eight hours ago, she would have had more of a chance of getting him to listen to her. Now she was tainted. Worse, he had seen her become tainted. Even worse, it was with Crank. Not only his best friend, but perhaps the sleaziest, dirtiest guy in Clover.

If he only knew the truth about Mindy...

If he only knew the truth about *anything*...

Fifty-nine

Once outside and not sure what to do, Doug walked to Whitney's house. He didn't know what he was going to say to her and he wasn't sure he was going to listen to her but... she *had* been right about the urn. But maybe that was just a guess. Maybe *she* had broken into his house and done something with the remaining ashes. But why would his mom have lied about that? Why wouldn't she have just said the ashes had been stolen for whatever reason?

There were a lot of questions that needed asking and Whitney seemed to be the only person eager to talk to him.

He approached her door, surprised he'd had to come this far. She had been so feverish in her attempts to contact him that he half-expected her to meet him outside.

He knocked on the door.

No answer.

Where could she be?

Probably out fucking Crank. Probably with every other slut in Clover.

Except Mindy.

Doug turned and looked around the quiet, empty neighborhood. It was only a matter of time before his mother made it out of the house or Deacon Pork came along and spotted him.

There was no answer at Whitney's house.

That meant there wasn't anyone inside.

Already he felt like he was backsliding, standing here and entertaining thoughts of breaking and entering, the only thing stopping him was what he remembered about Whitney's mom being a shut-in...

She also wasn't entirely well.

Maybe she was at a doctor's appointment or the hospital. Maybe that was where Whitney was, too.

Doug turned the knob. The door clicked. He wiped the knob with his shirt tail and pushed the door open with the cross.

The design of this house was the same as his. He walked through the small darkened foyer and came into the living room.

Whitney's mother was on the couch.

She wasn't alive.

It didn't look like she had been alive for a very long time.

A feeling of sadness for Whitney wriggled through Doug. Beneath that feeling was something more creeping and insidious.

Fear.

What the hell was going on?

He wanted to run out of the house screaming. He wanted to run out of Clover.

Instead, he went into the kitchen and sat down at the table, gently laying the metal cross on the dusty wood surface. The blinds were up and he could see his house from here.

Mindy said she would pick him up.

He waited for Mindy and tried to keep his nerves from rubberbanding around in his body.

He wondered if Whitney had any beer in her refrigerator.

Sixty

If there was a stage, Crank couldn't find it. They would have to use the truck. They had backed it in to unload all of the Duraflames and there wasn't any room to turn it around without driving it out of the cave. Crank felt too lazy to do that. He decided Patrick Crayze could set up his drums in the bed of the truck. Since it would be completely dark, exposure wasn't really an issue anyway. Lurk was already passed out in the cab, his head resting on the silent keyboard and Crank figured he could just stay there. Crank would play on the hood of the truck. Maybe he would sit down and rest his feet on the front bumper. Make it like a real acoustic, unplugged show. The impact of seeing them in this arrangement when the pyrotechnics went off would be awe inspiring.

Since Patrick Crayze would be closest to the logs, Crank gave him directions on lighting them. He set him up with a plastic jug of gas and a couple boxes of kitchen matches. After dousing the logs in gas, he was to light the matches and throw both boxes on the logs. Crank decided they should do this right before their final number, "Grandma Fisting."

As the last of the light faded from the mouth of the cave, Crank and Patrick Crayze went about their pre-show ritual of slapping each other in the ears. They were so drunk and high they couldn't feel anything. They kept smacking until the only thing they could hear was a high ringing. Crank thought this made their performance more real. Less reliant on fidelity and crowd approval.

He was a little nervous no one had come yet. But that wasn't a big deal. Sometimes they only played to the two or three people who'd heard about their show from the Internet and managed to crawl out of their parents' house long enough to check it out.

They finished setting up quickly and launched into their opener, "3 Balls Deep."

Crank couldn't hear if the crowd went wild or not.

He couldn't even tell if anyone was there.

He could barely hear his guitar.

After the first song, he'd have to tell Patrick Crayze to play a little softer.

Sixty-one

Doug sat at Whitney's kitchen table contemplating the web of lies woven around him. It seemed like anyone he'd ever been close to had done nothing but lie to him. How could he trust anyone anymore? Did every adult do this to everyone else? Were people just okay with it? Functioning in their own fabricated reality?

Even his own mother. He knew parents had to occasionally tell harmless lies to their children in order to shield them from the occasionally inevitable and ugly truth. But he thought there came a time in people's lives when they got to stop hearing those lies. How long would his mother have continued to lie to him about his father? And she still hadn't told him the truth. Even after confronting her.

Looking toward his house of lies now, he saw his mother exit. Maybe he should run out of the house, across the yard, and confront her again. But maybe he had scared her. Maybe she would call the police. Maybe he should take the cross and beat the truth out of her. It was a good metaphor.

He laughed quietly.

The cross.

Until only a few minutes ago, it had always been his father's urn.

He decided not to go over there.

He was going to sit where he was and wait for Mindy.

His mother got in the car and backed out of the driveway. Probably on her way to the Church.

Mindy.

Maybe she and Pastor Don were the only people who hadn't lied to him.

Since his mother had left, he probably didn't need to stay at Whitney's anyway.

She probably wouldn't be coming back any time soon. Probably at Crank's show. And then after the show they'd probably do God knew what. Doug had seen a couple of Crank's shows. He tried to look beyond the absence of God or Jesus in the lyrics and see how anyone could find it entertaining, but he thought it was all just an excuse for people to get together and party. He had tried to suspend judgment because he thought Crank had been his friend. But Crank wasn't his friend anymore and he didn't have to suspend judgment.

God's word was the only thing he believed in.

Crank's music was crap. He didn't even think that was a subjective critique. He just didn't think they were very talented, passionate, or knowledgeable.

If Doug were going to further his relationship with God, he needed to start being truthful with himself about these things. If there was one lesson he had learned from everyone's betrayal, it was that he was as much a part of this web of lies as they were.

He stood up from the table to go home, not even bothering to take the cross with him.

Once home, he sat in the darkened living room and waited for Mindy's horn.

Sixty-two

Whitney came out of the woods behind her house and went in through the back door. She went to the phone in the kitchen to call Doug at America Pantry again even though she was pretty sure he'd probably left.

The silver cross lay gleaming on the kitchen table.

Shit.

Doug or, even worse, his mother, had been here. That meant they knew about her mother.

Did it even matter?

In a few hours, would anything really matter ever again?

She put her hand on the cross and wondered if it had been left there as some kind of sign.

If Doug's mother had left it there, then it could be as some kind of threat. Like she knew what Whitney had told Doug about the urn. If that were the case, Whitney would probably be lucky to even be alive until midnight. It could still be an okay thing. If Doug *had* confronted his mother about the urn then it meant he still trusted Whitney a little. Maybe.

If Doug had left the urn there, then maybe it was as some kind of peace offering. Maybe he would listen to her now. Maybe he would believe her. Or maybe he'd come over to beat her to death with it.

Whitney picked up the cross and left through the front door.

As she stepped outside and turned to look toward Doug's house, she saw him getting into Mindy's car.

"Doug!" Whitney called.

He glanced at her, made a sour face, and flashed her a thumbs down.

Juvenile, she thought.

Something else. Just as Doug sat in the passenger seat and closed the door, she noticed Deacon Pork slide from the side of the house toward the car.

"Doug! Stop!"

But it was too late. Pork was in the car, quick and agile as a cat, and they were backing too fast into the street.

Whitney opened her garage door and pulled her bike down from the rack. She was finished with walking. She checked the bike's tires. Not perfect but she thought it would be okay to ride for a little while. She hopped on, wished she owned something besides dresses, put the long side of the cross between her legs so the cross bar rested on her thighs, and began pumping toward the Ark Sakura.

If she were lucky, they would all be so wasted when she got there that they would be ready to answer her call to arms and go fuck shit up. If she were even luckier, more than a couple people had turned out to watch them and they would be more than eager to join in.

It made her sad that Doug hadn't believed her. It meant she would have to be there and witness his face as all of his illusions were shattered. She had known the truth about the Church from an early age. But Doug had believed. It had been his passion for eighteen years. His entire life.

But it had to be done. She hoped there was some essential core to Doug's being that would realize this after the fact.

Sixty-three

Doug opened the passenger door and, despite Mindy's appearance, slid into the passenger seat.

Her head was shaved, her scalp gleaming white against the tan of her face. She wore a white robe that filled her half of the car. She looked like she had gained at least thirty pounds since the last time he had seen her and, even though she looked clean, a rank scent emanated from her.

He heard Whitney yell from her house and he turned to look at her, flashing a thumbs down.

"Hi Doug." Mindy smiled blissfully.

"Hi... uh, Mindy."

The back door opened and Doug felt something sting him on the neck. He tried to swat it away but it was already gone.

Or that spot was numb. He didn't even feel his hand make contact with his neck.

Or his neck was numb.

His whole body felt numb.

He tried to ask Mindy if she had seen what it was that had bitten him but his mouth wouldn't work. He didn't even have the chance to think something really bad was happening to him before he plummeted into unconsciousness.

Sixty-four

Officer Viled kept his hand up Amanda's skirt on the ride to the Church. More specifically, he kept his fingers in her vagina. Plunging in and out until she worked up some come and then smelling his fingers.

It was only about a ten minute ride but, halfway there, he pulled the car off the road. He told her to get out of the car and down on all fours. He grabbed some lube from the glove compartment. He dropped to his knees behind her, unfastened his pants, hiked up her skirt, tugged down her damp underwear and plunged into her. He opened the lube and coated his right hand with it. Slowly, he worked his fingers into Amanda's ass before eventually making a fist and sliding his arm in to mid-forearm.

Amanda bucked against him. She'd never felt anything like this. She loved it.

They continued well after sundown. Amanda could see the lights crawling over them from other cars on their way to the Church, to the ceremony. She liked this too. She didn't know how many people in the cars were actually able to see them. She hoped it was a lot. She wanted them to see her down on all fours like a dog, a practical stranger's arm up her ass while she drooled with pleasure into the gravel on the side of the road. She wanted the men to fantasize about being the one pounding into her. She wanted the women to pretend to be her—away from their homes, away from their husbands and children with nothing but the pain, pleasure, and lingering humiliation of this act.

Because in a very short while, she would be standing in front of them and telling them what she had seen.

She would tell them about the Beast, about their Lord. And she would tell them about the Becoming. She would tell them about how everything Pastor Don had promised them was true.

And then the true face of the Beast would be revealed and they would all witness it together.

She saw this in a revelatory flash as an orgasm slammed through her body, her sphincter restricting on Viled's arm until he pulled it out with a wet slurp.

She'd seen the Beast's true face.

And it was up to her to bring this person forward.

To drink and bathe in the blood of the virgin.

Sixty-five

Crank signaled to Patrick Crayze to launch into their final number and then realized he couldn't see him so he played the opening chords. Patrick Crayze didn't immediately kick in with the drums which could have meant his ear drums were completely blown and he hadn't heard him or he was too high and drunk and couldn't figure out what Crank was playing yet or he'd remembered what he was supposed to do and was at this very moment dousing a thousand plus Duraflames with gasoline.

A few seconds later a hellish blaze erupted behind Crank. The heat was tremendous. In the glow he saw more faces in front of him than he'd ever seen at a show. There must have been a hundred.

And they all looked completely terrified.

Crank dropped the guitar and leapt off the truck, carried with the herd of panicked, screaming teenagers as the flames jetted toward the mouth of the cave.

Patrick Crayze was killed instantly and was pretty sure he'd seen God.

Lurk had actually been dead for the past hour so he didn't feel the heat explode the blood in his veins and curl his skin inward.

Any of the audience members who had stumbled on their way out of the cave, if not already trampled to death, were burned alive.

Not entirely aware of the seriousness of the situation, Crank raised his hand into a fist and shouted, "White trash pyrotechnics! Chainsaw Enema forever!"

A lot of other people, unaware that Chainsaw Enema no longer existed, took up the chant along with other assorted yelps and hoots.

And then there was the crazy girl on the bike with the cross and it just kept being the best night ever.

Sixty-six

Luckily the Ark Sakura was in the hollow so it was a mostly downhill coast from Whitney's. She managed to make it almost all the way there before dark. She didn't think she would be riding the bike anywhere else tonight. Despite the nearly full moon, the hollow would still be pitch black.

She wasn't exactly sure where it was until she saw a jet of fire shoot up into the air.

The fact that Crank was a huge fucking idiot again reinforced itself to her.

She followed the jet of fire and the frantic screams.

When she finally came upon the opening to the Ark, she was amazed at the amount of people gathering around what had become the biggest bonfire she'd ever seen. She wasn't sure if it had blown the top of the cave off, escaped through an opening, or simply spread with such intensity that the woods on all surrounding sides of the cave were burning.

It was that wild energy in the air. That was the only thing she could think to explain this amount of people attending one of Crank's shows. She needed to find a way to harness that energy. She had to think fast.

She stayed on the bike and hoisted the cross up high and upside down with her right hand.

Sixty-seven

Crank looked at the girl on the bike and it took him a few seconds to realize it was Whitney. The bright intensity of the fire made the dark that much darker.

She pulled her bike to a stop and lifted that crazy urn Doug always thought held his father. She bellowed, "Listen up! Don't let this moment pass us by! The Church is full of everything that makes this place awful! Let's storm it! Let's storm the Church!"

Maybe it was just the excitement of everything that had been happening, but Crank felt something as close to love as he'd ever felt before.

He raised both fists above his head and shouted, "Let's do what she said! Let's storm the fucking Church!"

Crank thought that sounded way beyond arena rock. He thought it sounded totally black metal.

Whitney hopped off the bike, continuing to brandish the cross. Crank didn't know if it was due to the intense heat of their surroundings or if he'd actually begun hallucinating from all the pills, but it looked like the cross was glowing orange.

The group left en masse with Whitney and Crank in the lead. Behind them the forest burned.

Sixty-eight

By the time Amanda and Viled reached the Church, it was already packed. They opened the doors and everyone turned to look at them. Viled whispered seductively into her ear that he was going to the restroom to "wash all the shit off his hand."

She was surprised to see Pastor Don beaming down at her from the pulpit. A boy lay on his back, seemingly unconscious, on the altar in front of it. She thought it was the Backus kid.

"Amanda," Pastor Don said.

She was too overwhelmed to speak. She could only blush and smile broadly.

"Our witness has returned. Now we may begin."

Amanda started trying to find an empty space in the pews but Pastor Don stopped her.

"We wouldn't dream of having our witness sit amongst the masses! You'll come and stand next to me. Your time to speak is near at hand."

Amanda loved Pastor Don's way with words. Sometimes the things he said sounded like they came right out of the Bible. She practically floated to the front of the Church.

"That's it! Don't be nervous!"

She ascended the two steps and stood next to Pastor Don. He reached out and gave her a playful smack on the ass. Amanda was afraid the impact would make something dribble out.

She looked out at the congregation. She wasn't in any state to fully dwell on it but she'd never really given a thought to Clover's peculiar demographic until now. There were probably 300 people in the congregation. She saw only three men, one of whom was the unconscious one on the altar. Five altogether if you counted Pastor Larsta and Officer Viled, who still hadn't returned from the restrooms.

"Dear flock," Pastor Don began. "We are at the end of an eighteen year journey. Glory glory. Yet, we are at the beginning of an eternal one."

Amanda noticed the initiates in the front row, staring toward them with a combination of rapture and hunger.

"Before me lay young Doug Backus. But as we enter the depth of the summer solstice, he will cease to become Doug Backus. What he will become is a vessel of life. A vessel that we must drink from."

There was a smattering of applause.

"But he's not just a vessel. He's also a key. His blood, the purest blood born at the exact right time, will transform our Lord permanently. Our Lord has hungers, he has needs, and in order to lead us, in order to make us as powerful as him, he must be transformed. No more will the innocents fall victim to his ravenous powers. From this day forward we will go out into the world, we will convert the nonbelievers. They will see the power of our Lord and they will welcome this transformation... Or they will die."

The congregation held its applause but most of them smiled broadly.

"To carry our word to the rest of the world, our initiates have been preparing diligently. Please stand."

Mindy, Angie, and Kristen all stood.

Pastor Don announced their names and said, "Our witness has

watched over their diligent preparations, as well."

Pastor Don performed a combination pat and caress on her ass and Amanda, thinking she was supposed to say something, yelled, "And the blood did flow!"

Now the congregation laughed and applauded softly.

"Well, we know why you all came here this evening so I won't draw the suspense out any longer. You all want to know who the Great Beast is!"

Now they clapped wildly.

"You all want to know who your leader is!"

Continued clapping, whistles and hoots.

"Our witness is here to tell you!"

Lengthy applause slowly dying down to complete silence.

"Amanda? Who amongst the congregation has been silently leading us this entire time? Who amongst us has grown restless and hungry?"

Amanda searched the congregation. She didn't know. She didn't know who it was supposed to be. Officer Viled's name popped into her head but that didn't seem right either. Pastor Don's name was there, too, but that seemed to... obvious, maybe.

"Who will help us turn the corner into paradise? Glory glory. Who will give birth to hell as they did a child without a mate!"

Amanda continued to scan the crowd. She needed to say a name. She needed to rely on her faith. If she *truly* had faith and she truly *was* the chosen witness, then whatever answer she gave would be correct, wouldn't it?

The name popped into her head and she shouted, "Martha Backus!"

At the sound of her name, the burly woman rose from the second pew and came forward.

Amanda knew from the overwhelming response that she had chosen correctly. When she looked over at Pastor Don, he beamed at her.

"Glory glory!" he shouted.

"Glory glory!" she shouted back.

"Glory glory!" Martha Backus shouted.

Pastor Don reached into the pulpit and pulled out a large curved knife. It looked like the same one she had seen the initiates use in the Tabernacle. He held the blade and brandished the haft of the knife toward her. Amanda took the knife and was immediately ready to pounce on Doug Backus, slice his throat open, dance around in his blood.

"Glory glory," Pastor Don said. "Get a feel for that knife and, at the stroke of midnight, when the time comes, you will do the job. You will be the maker of the ultimate sacrifice." He held his hand back out for the knife. "Until *then* we will witness the transformation and celebrate the initiates' graduation from the Tabernacle." With his free hand he delicately grabbed her chin. "You remember how we celebrate, don't ya, honey?"

Now she was virtually ecstatic. "Oh, yes, I've been celebrating for days." The congregation laughed and applauded.

Pastor Don descended the steps and kneeled in front of the altar. He carved an upside down cross on Doug's forehead and dipped each of his fingertips into the blood before pressing his palm onto Doug's forehead. He stood up and held his red right hand toward the congregation.

"Behold!" he shouted.

Now Martha Backus was in front of him in what Amanda thought was almost a sex position. Pastor Don pressed his bloody palm to her forehead and everyone watched the transformation.

Martha stood. Her body became even larger. Horns sprouted from her head. Her mouth filled with teeth. Her clothes fell away in tatters. A tail dangled at the back of her legs. An enormous penis dangled from the front.

"And now ladies of the congregation, come forth and accept the blood of the sacrifice and the seed of the Beast. Be one with the Church of the New Covenant!"

The congregation erupted into the same frenzied sexual activity she remembered from before. The difference this time was the steady line of females coming forth to lie on Doug while the Beast serviced them, straining their vaginas, filling them with semen to the point that it spilled out on the sacrifice until he was covered in blood and semen.

They fucked frantically toward midnight.

Sixty-nine

Whitney liked the feeling of being followed by a group of drunken teenagers who would do anything she told them to. They were all covered in sweat and they smelled like fire.

"Is it midnight yet?" Whitney asked Crank.

"I don't know. I don't have a watch."

"Maybe your phone?"

"Really?" He pulled it out of his pocket, looked at the glowing 11:42 on it and said, "Hm."

"There's still time."

She could see the Church in front of them. The parking lot was filled with cars. They bled out onto the street. Whitney thought they'd be able to just walk in. She didn't think churches locked their doors provided there was anyone in there. Still holding the cross in her right hand, she pulled on the door handle with her left.

Locked.

That only reaffirmed her belief they were doing something nefarious in there. At a temporary loss for what to do, she knocked on the door. She heard voices from inside but no one answered.

She took the cross in both hands and began hammering it against the door.

She sensed Crank and the others becoming restless.

"Um... what should we do?" Crank asked.

"I don't know... Bust out some windows. Trash some cars. Set stuff on fire!"

It was like letting loose a pack of wild dogs. Windows immediately shattered. The church van exploded, shooting at least ten feet into the air before coming down in a blackened, smoldering heap.

Once the chaos was in full swing, the church doors opened.

Whitney now stood face to face with Deacon Pork. Before he punched her in the face, she had the chance to look past him and into the Church. She wasn't exactly sure what she expected to see but people fucking everywhere was certainly not it. But then again, in a town that encourages its girls to fuck a monster, she probably shouldn't have been that surprised. The fist hit her before she could locate Doug. There was the pop of her nose that immediately began running blood and swelling to the size of a sausage and a bright flash from the middle of her head, but she didn't go down. Instead, she rocked back with the cross and drove it into Deacon Pork's head.

His head exploded in blood and brain matter.

That probably shouldn't have happened.

Rather than stopping to think about it, she continued to charge forward.

The other people at Crank's show were now coming in through the windows. Many of them seemed confused, took off their clothes, and joined in.

Then, at the front of the Church, Whitney saw it.

Or her.

Or... him.

The Beast.

The one she had tracked to Doug's house so long ago.

Doug's mother.

Mrs. Backus.

The one who her own mother had wanted Whitney to couple

with upon entering high school. Whitney had refused and been removed from the town. Sent to the nearest psychiatric facility. But they couldn't keep her there once she turned eighteen. So she'd come home to find her mother dead on the couch. That was good, in a way. It allowed Whitney to convince herself that her mother did love her, that she would have gotten her out of the hospital sooner if she'd been alive.

"You!"

It was that whore Mindy. Another one of the chosen. One who'd either said yes to the degradation of the Beast or who didn't have the spine to say no to her mother.

"Where's Doug?" Whitney said.

Mindy, looking bald, fat, and hideous, smiled and said, "See for yourself."

Doug lay on the altar at the front of the Church. A woman lay on top of him. The Beast thrust into the woman.

Whitney struck with the cross. It hit Mindy in the shoulder and her arm fell off, blood shooting from the newly created cavity.

"Get this bitch!" Mindy shouted.

Whitney struck with the cross again. This time it hit Mindy in the head. Her head exploded. Whitney felt a brief moment of victory before the lights in the Church went out.

There were hands all over. Some of them tried to hurt her. Some of them tried to rip her clothes off. Some of them did both. Even more frightening than the lights going out was that she could still see. The night outside the windows glowed a hellish orange. She smelled smoke coming in from the windows.

Seventy

Before the lights went out, Amanda saw a lot of new people coming in. They seemed even younger and more virile than most of the congregation who'd made it there on time. Amanda welcomed them and they seemed to be glad. One of their cocks was in her mouth, one of them was in her cunt, and yet a third was in her ass. She didn't know how they managed to make it work and she didn't care. She felt like she was going to explode. She tried to cry out but her mouth was full.

Then the lights went out only... maybe they didn't?

The Church still glowed. A hellish orange. Amanda didn't know if she was supposed to be happy about that or not. She felt happy right now.

Maybe that was all that mattered.

She felt ecstatic.

Then she heard gunshots and felt that Officer Viled had finally made it out of the bathroom.

Seventy-one

Crank didn't feel really scared until the gunshots started. He didn't know where they were coming from. He needed to find Whitney and see if she knew where Doug was. He grabbed a hymnal or a Bible or whatever the fuck it was and started smacking at people, hoping he would catch a glint from Whitney's cross.

He thought he could *hear* it.

Bullets ricocheting off the steel.

He looked to see who was doing the shooting.

Silhouetted against the glow from outside, he thought he saw him.

Officer Viled.

Not a surprise.

He was within arm's reach.

Standing there with his pants off and smelling like sex and shit and just *unloading* that gun into the crowd.

And maybe Whitney was somewhere in the middle of all that.

Crank began hitting Officer Viled in the head with the spine of the book.

It must have surprised him enough to get him to drop the gun. Crank picked it up, having absolutely no idea how it worked, and charged toward the crowd.

Something giant and stinking ran past him.

He plunged his arm into the group of people, past all the sweaty flesh and, when he felt burning metal, he latched on and pulled with everything he had, which wasn't very much.

Seventy-two

Since first seeing Doug, Whitney hadn't taken her eyes from him. She was knocked onto her back. She kept one hand on the cross, hacking away as much as she could. Her clothes had been torn from her body. Someone was between her legs, going to town. Since she wasn't wet in the least, it hurt and tore more than anything. Then she watched as the Beast grabbed Doug and charged for the front door. Some asshole had grabbed onto the cross and wouldn't let go. Whitney wasn't about to let go either. She felt herself being dragged down the aisle. The penis that had been violating her slid out and thrust increasingly farther down her leg. She stomped her foot when she thought it would be about there. Hopefully she damaged him in some way.

She scrambled to her feet and stood face to face with Crank.

"Crank!"

"Yeah, you can thank me later. Know where Doug is?"

Whitney quickly assessed where they were. They were at the wrong end now. Near the pulpit.

"They're gone," Whitney said.

"Gone?"

"Out the front door."

"Shit."

Whitney noticed Pastor Don Larsta slouched and naked, resting a hand against the pulpit. He looked like a man whose dreams just died and, Whitney guessed, he kind of was.

"Hang on," she told Crank. She hoisted the cross high and brought it down on the unsuspecting pastor's skull.

His head exploded at about the same time as the western wall of the Church erupted into flame.

"Good work!" Crank said.

"There has to be a door back here somewhere."

They found a door and stormed toward the front of the Church. Whitney looked for tracks. She'd tracked the Beast before. She felt like she had its scent now. She told Crank to follow her and then asked him what time it was.

"11:55."

Seventy-three

Doug opened his eyes. It didn't really feel like he had woken up. It felt more like he kept *trying* to wake up. There was this constant movement that made him feel like he wanted to throw up. He felt so weak. Too weak to even get out of bed.

But he wasn't in his bed.

Where was he?

The hospital?

The last thing he remembered was getting stung in Mindy's car and then...

What?

Nothing.

So where was he now?

The first thought he had was that he was being carried by a giant.

Then he remembered the beast that had pinned him down that one night in the woods. His test of faith. But he thought he'd been good enough since then. Perhaps he'd been too harsh in his judgments of Crank and Whitney.

Why was he even thinking about any of this? He should be trying to get away.

But there was no strength.

He felt damp and weak and sick.

Drugged. Exhausted.

He gave everything he had and flailed his body. Whatever was carrying him came to a shuddering stop to better secure its hold before picking up the trot again.

He thought he heard a voice calling from behind him.

Two voices.

Crank and Whitney...

Seventy-four

"Doug!" Whitney yelled.

"Hang in there," Crank rasped. The cigarette and pot smoking had not been kind to his lungs.

Whitney saw where they were headed.

The Tabernacle.

That was where her mother had wanted her to go. Part of Whitney had wanted to go just to find out what went on in there. But she had trusted the rumors. More importantly, she had trusted her instincts. Whatever happened in there was probably terrible.

The Beast burst through the door.

Seventy-five

And dropped Doug onto the sticky stinking floor. Doug looked up into the eyes of the Beast and thought he saw something familiar. Wherever they were, it smelled like the Beast times a thousand.

The Beast dropped to its knees and straddled Doug.

He didn't have the strength or the will power to even try to kick it off.

So this is how it ends, he thought. It seemed appropriate. Just a pointless act of violence between him and a creature he didn't even understand. Something that came from the bowels of hell. Something that was pure evil.

And evil was going to win again.

And so it was here as it was all over the world.

He closed his eyes and waited for the death blow.

Seventy-six

Whitney hit the doorway and didn't even pause as the stink smacked into her.

The Beast's claws were headed straight for Doug's already damaged neck.

Whitney threw the cross with everything she had.

The Beast was so filled with bloodlust it didn't even look up.

The cross didn't hit the arm that Whitney had aimed for.

It hit the Beast in the skull and its head exploded, a rain of blood and gore spilling down onto Doug.

He didn't even try to wriggle out from under the corpse.

Crank approached the Beast and kicked it off Doug. Now lifeless, the body began to revert back to the form of Doug's mother but, without the head, it was mostly unrecognizable.

Saturday, June 21st

Seventy-seven

Doug waited for the blow that never came. He felt the weight of the Beast on his body. He heard a victorious cheer from Crank and Whitney.

He kept his eyes closed and let unconsciousness take him once again.

He felt safe.

He felt loved.

Seventy-eight

"We have to get him out of here," Whitney said.

And it was true. The fire still raged outside.

Whitney grabbed his arms and Crank grabbed his legs. They walked quickly, not entirely sure where they were going.

Seventy-nine

Around one, they came to America Pantry.

"Shit, Patel's here," Crank said. "You stay out here with Doug."

Crank opened the door and walked into the brightly lighted store.

"Hey, Mr. Patel, I'm here for my shift."

Patel looked surprised. "First time in three days, yes? And you're not wearing the shirt I made you. And you look like dog shit and stink a lot. Know what I think? I think you and your friend are both bullshitters. I think this town is all bullshitters. All crazy."

"Well, yeah..."

"I also think you're in trouble." Patel moved his right hand and for a horrified instant, Crank was sure he was going to grab his gun and shoot him. But he was just reaching for the register. The drawer slid open. Patel emptied it and put the pile of cash on the counter. "You take this," he said. "Get help." Next to the pile of cash he placed the keys to his Mercedes. "And take that. I'm going to call my wife and she will bring the children and we will drive very far away from here. Collect insurance and laugh like loonies."

He pointed at the television. Aerial footage of the fire engulfing Clover.

Crank didn't think he'd heard about Clover on the news for anything other than school cancelations and delays.

Crank took the money and the keys.

"Thank you, Mr. Patel."

Mr. Patel laughed. As Crank was leaving Patel said, "I hope that wasn't caused by a thousand and three Duraflame logs."

"A thousand and six," Crank said. "The inventory was off."

He went out into the glowing night.

Eighty

Doug awoke in a motel room sometime the next afternoon.

Crank was asleep in the other bed, exhausted from driving all night. The only question had been whether to go north or south. They had chosen south. Decided they would try and find work in Florida and monitor the news from Clover. If their names were never mentioned, maybe they'd stay in the States, maybe they'd stay together. If any authorities were looking for them, they'd hire a boat to take them to some island in the Caribbean. After what they'd been through, they felt like they could do anything.

That left Whitney to explain to Doug what had happened.

Almost before she even started he apologized to her, told her he knew. Knew that his real father was out there.

Whitney almost considered letting him have this belief. Letting him believe his mother had died in the fire and his real father was still out there.

But she couldn't.

She couldn't because he had been lied to his entire life and it was time for that to stop.

Besides, in the end, maybe a person's quest for religion is really just that person wanting to believe that magic exists.

And she had a magical story for him.

Eighty-one

Doug lay on the bed and listened to Whitney's crazy story about Clover and the people who ran it. About how every eighteen years there was a child born to a woman without the act of intercourse. How that woman became a beast. An incarnation of Satan himself. And about how they had to go out and hunt, killing the men of the town and fucking the women, which made most people in the town related.

She told him about the one special child, usually a male, who had to be kept a virgin until the summer solstice of his eighteenth year. And how that virgin would then be sacrificed so the Beast could keep its Satanic form.

How they performed the same ritual every eighteen years and never made it work.

But this time it was close. Closer than ever.

She reduced his life to something that took less than an hour. It explained everything. The fake religion. His mother's protectiveness. Even the crazy lust of the women on what was almost his last day on earth. They sensed the power.

If that was what his mother had been, then what did that make him?

He felt, somehow, special... and realized he didn't want to be.

Listening to Whitney talk, he didn't know if he should believe her or not.

He didn't really know what to believe and there was something that opened in his mind or his soul and told him he didn't have to believe in anything at all.

Doug felt his entire body relax with this knowledge.

He could believe nothing or he could believe anything he felt like believing which was maybe everything.

All of it.

Doug smiled.

He felt like he was starting at the beginning.

It was a pretty great feeling.

Other Grindhouse Press Titles

#011 – *Pray You Die Alone: Horror Stories*
by Andersen Prunty

#010 – *King of the Perverts*
by Steve Lowe

#009 – *Sunruined: Horror Stories*
by Andersen Prunty

#008 – *Bright Black Moon: Vampires in Devil Town Book Two*
by Wayne Hixon

#007 – *Hi I'm a Social Disease: Horror Stories*
by Andersen Prunty

#006 – *A Life On Fire*
by Chris Bowsman

#005 – *The Sorrow King*
by Andersen Prunty

#004 – *The Brothers Crunk*
by William Pauley III

#003 – *The Horribles*
by Nathaniel Lambert

#002 – *Vampires in Devil Town*
by Wayne Hixon

#001 – *House of Fallen Trees*
by Gina Ranalli

#000 – *Morning is Dead*
by Andersen Prunty

Manufactured by Amazon.ca
Bolton, ON